UNDER THE MOUNTAIN

J.P. CHOQUETTE

UNDER THE MOUNTAIN

J.P. Choquette

OTHER BOOKS BY J.P. CHOQUETTE

Published by: Scared E Cat Books

Cover design: Bespoke Book Covers

ISBN: ISBN: 978-1-950976-04-1

For Pascal, who loves wild places and has the heart of an adventurer.
Your zest for life inspires everyone around you. I love you more than you can imagine.

1

GRACELYN EDWARDS

START OF DIABLO POINT TRAIL

Present Day

"You're being stupid, Gracie. This isn't a good idea."

Gracelyn Edwards closed her eyes.

"Let the words flow over you, like water off a duck," her therapist had told her more than once. "They can't hurt you unless you believe them and let them in."

But Roger's words stung. There was no "flow" when your brother called you stupid, let alone tried to bully you out of doing what had to be done.

Gracelyn let a few choice words roll around in her head before speaking. When she did, hand on the truck's door handle, it was brief and to the point.

"I'm going. I need this."

Roger shook his head, looked off into the distance through the smeared windshield. "I think this is about the worst idea you've ever had. Haven't you put Mom through enough? Are you trying to kill her?"

This cut like acid through Gracelyn's heart. She took a deep breath through her nose like she'd been taught. Slowly, to the count of four. Then hold it for another count of four, then release it to yet another count of four and hold once more. Square breathing, Addie called it. For times when Gracelyn couldn't cope. When her nerves and that loud voice in her head took over.

"I'll see you on Sunday, Rog. Thanks for the ride." She got out of the dented truck and walked around to the back. She was half sure that Roger would drive away with her backpack, just to prove his point. Instead, he sat stiffly in the driver's seat.

Gracelyn struggled to pull the pack free of the truck's bed. A strap must have gotten jammed under the cap somehow. She felt around with her hands in the dark interior, found where the strap had gotten caught and then pulled, trying to dislodge it without having to climb into the truck's bed. Roger's door opened and seconds later Gracelyn felt his calloused hands on her upper arms.

"Here, let me get it." He nudged her out of the way and freed the strap, then pushed the pack toward her. She reached for it but he didn't let go.

"Sure you won't reconsider?" His voice was softer, less gruff.

Gracelyn shook her head, avoiding her brother's eyes. The slick nylon pack felt slippery.

"Here," he shoved it the rest of the way into her hands. She wobbled a little at the sudden weight of it, but straightened quickly, not wanting Roger to see that he'd gotten her off balance. In more ways than one.

"See you Sunday," she repeated. He grunted a response. Gracelyn hefted the pack over her shoulders and tried not to stagger under the weight. She'd packed too much, she knew that. But it was her first time out since...well, in a long time. And she hadn't wanted to leave behind anything important.

She felt Roger's eyes on her back as she crossed the road and stepped into the woods. She walked to the trailhead-that-wasn't. Diablo Point was where she was headed, a mountain deep in the Green Mountain National Forest. The trail wasn't marked because it wasn't supposed to exist. Tightening her grip on her walking stick, Gracelyn glanced back over her shoulder. Roger was leaning on the truck, crossed arms resting on his thick barrel belly. He lifted a hand in a wave.

"Sunday," he called out before adjusting his cap and walking back to the driver's side door. "And Gracie?" his voice carried on the light breeze that had picked up. "Be careful out there."

ROGER'S WORDS wound themselves through Gracelyn's brain. Every step she took kept tempo with the words. Right foot...*be careful*...left foot...*out there. Be careful...out there.* The more she tried to push the words away the louder they beat like a drum in her head. They drowned out the sounds of the pileated woodpecker overhead, boasting in its extra-loud trill. The words muted the whisper of the tree leaves and muffled the sound of the first babbling brook that Gracelyn crossed. She was so caught up in her thoughts that when her right foot slipped off the slick log suspended over the brook, it startled her. The icy cold mountain water soaked the top of the lucky red sock that peeked out of her hiking boot.

The trail—if you could call it that—was badly over-grown. Since the town below it had been abandoned, the trail had fallen into disrepair. Diablo Point had never been part of the Long Trail which wound its way over the spine of Vermont. This trail, it was said, had been used as a shortcut by townspeople long ago. It had been worn away by many feet at first. Later, groups of hardy men had carved it with axes and scythes and God knew what else.

Gracelyn couldn't imagine that a steep path like this over a mountain of over three thousand feet would be used by anyone as a shortcut. The nearest town lay just on the other side though or had at one point. Now it too had been mostly abandoned. A few trailers and tar-paper covered cabins remained in use.

After hiking another hour, Gracelyn stopped to check both the map and compass needlessly. She drew both close to her face, making sure she hadn't missed anything. Her hands shook. Despite not having coffee that morning, she was jittery. The woods—nature—had always been the one part of life where she felt peaceful, where she could be the truest version of herself. She closed her eyes, tried to bring to mind some of the happiest times she'd spent in the wild. Instead, other memories came to mind, ones she wished could be deleted. Images of that day two years ago. Her father. The tunnel. The snake—

A branch cracked nearby and Gracelyn turned, eyes scanning the forest around her. But everything looked the same as it had before: slightly dim, fuzzy leaves overhead, muted shades of greens and browns and grays. A tiny figure scurried from a nearby log—a chipmunk or squirrel probably—other than that nothing moved. The hair at the base of her neck stood up though. She could feel eyes on her. Carefully she scanned the forest again but didn't see anything human or animal.

It was mid-July. The heat of the day was only hours

away. If Gracelyn hoped to be resting around lunchtime, she needed to get moving. She replaced the map and compass in her pack and pulled the straps over her shoulders again.

Far away a bird tweeted furiously and closer, a portly bumblebee lurched drunkenly around some flowers. The wind sighed through pine tree boughs. Focusing on these noises helped Gracelyn to quiet that other voice in her head, the one stuck on *be careful...out there* and she was grateful. Ever since the...the accident, she'd had trouble drowning out the voice. Anxiety. Worry. Fear.

Addie, her therapist, had told her that these feelings took many different guises. For Gracelyn it was all strange and unfamiliar territory. She'd never understood people scared of doing things or who fretted over decisions. You decided what to do and did it, simple as that. But now, things were different. Anxiety clung to her like a sticky shawl. The confidence that had always come so easily had crept away, beaten down by this voice in her head. She hated it.

The sound of talking cut through her thoughts. Gracelyn paused. She must be hearing things. No one came up here. But seconds later she heard the voices again: the low rumble of a man and the higher response of a woman. There was a bright splash of red and a darker blue behind it. Then two figures appeared on the trail above her, descending.

"Oh, hello," the woman, blonde-haired and friendly-faced said. "Beautiful day, isn't it?" Then without waiting for an answer. "Surprised to see you here. I didn't think anyone used this old path anymore."

"First time," Gracelyn lied.

The woman stopped in the trail, causing the man behind her to bump into her.

"Sorry," he said, then glanced at Gracelyn. "How are you?"

"Good. Where are you coming from?"

"Hidden Lake," the woman answered. "Shh," she put a finger to her lips. "We were skinny dipping."

"Water's icy but very refreshing," the man said. "Heading up there?" He fished a bandana out of his pocket and wiped it over his face.

"No. A little higher."

"Alone?" the woman asked.

"No, I'm, um, meeting some friends."

"That's good. Not safe for a woman to be out here alone. You hear too many horror stories of kidnappings...and worse." She paused, pushed at her curls with the back of her hand. Her next question caught Gracelyn off guard.

"You're not one of those paranormal people are you?"

"Come on, hon," the man interrupted and stuffed the bandana back into his pocket.

"Paranormal people?" Gracelyn asked.

The woman shook her head. "There's been a lot of that around here...since. Well. After that tragedy—"

"We'd better keep moving." The man interrupted again. "We'll lose daylight before we hit Cross Peak if we don't." Then to Gracelyn, "We've got another peak to bag before we crash tonight. You have a great time."

Gracelyn forced her lips into a smile and nodded.

"Yes, have fun and be safe," the woman said. "Oh, and keep an eye out for the snake," she said in a stage whisper.

Gracelyn's smile slipped.

The man nudged her. "Come on, hon. And please stop with the snake stories." He rolled his eyes at Gracelyn. "It's just an old legend."

"It's not," the woman argued, swatting his arm. "It's been

recorded many times over the years. There have been accounts of it as far back as the early 1800s and—"

"I've heard about it," Gracelyn interrupted. "Sorry, I don't mean to be rude but I've got to push on. I don't want to be late meeting my friends."

The woman looked surprised to be interrupted, but the man's mouth turned up in a smile.

"Have a good hike," Gracelyn said.

"Sure, you too," the woman said.

"Hon," the man repeated and the woman slowly started descending. Gracelyn could feel her looking back up at her but pretended not to notice.

Everyone who grew up around here knew about the snake. Gracelyn and her friends used to talk about it in school, several swearing to have seen it on the outskirts of town. Never mind that Bondville was nearly twenty miles to the east of Diablo Point.

The snake had crossed a road, one of her classmates had said. He'd seen it coming home from his farm job on the other side of town, late at night. Another had sworn that she and her brother had seen it slither out of the water at a popular swimming hole. Other accounts dotted the landscape of the village, so many that it became ridiculous. Over time, the snake became the scapegoat for everything bad in Bondville.

When the crabby old woman who lived on the side of the mountain lost her dog, the town blamed it on the snake. When tourists overturned their kayaks on the still lake? The snake must have done it. When cats went missing or trees fell unexpectedly, toppling over roots and all, the snake was said to have caused the trouble.

They'd dared each other as teenagers to stay up at the top of the mountain—an inhospitable spot—and try to call out the snake. They'd joked about snake charmers and special music played on wooden flutes and learning ancient languages.

It had been easy to laugh it off then. Sitting around a fire with warm cans of soda and bright stars twinkling overhead. And it had stayed easy until she and her father had climbed this mountain together. It was two years ago this month when Gracelyn's entire world had shifted. When it had gone from turning smoothly on its axis to grinding to a standstill.

All because of one choice. One stupid decision.

Gracelyn shivered suddenly, the air too cool on her damp skin. When she swallowed her throat and mouth were dry. She didn't bother pulling out her canteen, though. Instead, she yanked her pack straps tighter and continued up the trail.

2

SHAWN EDWARDS

START OF DIABLO POINT TRAIL

Two Years Ago

"All set, Gracie?" Shawn double-checked his pockets one more time and waited for the "uh-huh" from his daughter before shutting and locking the cab of the pickup. It would be three days before they returned and he didn't want to risk local hooligans or raccoons getting inside.

Tucking the keys into his pocket, he hefted his pack and felt his leg muscles all struggle to adjust for the extra weight. When he turned toward the woods, Gracelyn was already ahead of him. She always was. The pack on her shoulders was big and she stood slightly hunched against its weight.

"Sure you don't want me to take the camp stove?"

She shook her head just like she had the last time he'd asked.

"Nope. I've got it. Let's go."

He smiled at her retreating back. She was like a racehorse, all full of nervous energy. He remembered that from his own youth. What it had felt like to hike trails you'd never been on, wondering what was around the next corner, over the next knoll. At fifty-eight, he didn't like to think that those days or experiences were behind him. They just came less frequently than they used to.

They crossed the road and got to the start of Diablo Point Trail. There was no sign but locals knew it by sight.

"Think it'll rain?" she asked over her shoulder.

Shawn looked up. Dark smudges of clouds littered the sky. A cool breeze was coming in from the east.

"Dunno. Maybe."

Gracelyn didn't respond and Shawn hurried forward so he could keep her in sight. Keeping Gracelyn in his sight had been a full-time job for a long time. Since she was big enough to crawl she'd been getting into mischief. She'd been the baby who had refused naps, spending the time instead finding ingenious ways out of her crib. He'd called an end to naps when she'd managed to shimmy down the crib's leg at just over a year old. Gracelyn had been the first of the two kids to walk, had skipped the crawling stage altogether. She'd been the first to fall out of a tree, first to break her arm, first to need stitches—not all on the same day, thankfully.

Roger was older and bigger than his sister, but it was Gracelyn who was in charge as soon as she was old enough to talk. She'd bossed Roger when they were kids and she hadn't stopped giving him "suggestions", since. Roger shouldn't use the farm for dairy cows anymore, Gracelyn told him repeatedly. The real future was in organic produce. Never mind that the farm had had cows on it since three generations back or that Roger loved working with the slow-moving animals. Roger should look into permaculture practices. It was the wave of the future. If he insisted on keeping cows, Roger should start a Community Supported Agriculture program—a CSA—and offer his milk and cheese at a discount to those who signed up. Had he considered upscale products like artisan cheeses and flavored whey products?

Gracelyn herself had been through more jobs that Shawn could keep track of. She'd been a receptionist, worked at a lighting store, sold fish out of the back of a pickup truck one summer when she moved to Maine on a whim. She'd tried her hand at pottery and thought at one point she wanted to be a musician—though she could barely carry a tune and her instrument of choice was a harmonica. There was little that deterred her.

Like this trip. She and Shawn had wanted to take a four-day weekend trip. One last hurrah to summer before Gracelyn left to go out West. Thankfully, she'd given up on the idea of a career in music. Instead, she'd become a freelance investigative journalist. At least, that's what she called herself. She had a blog—some sort of website from what Shawn gathered—where she shared stories of strange happenings, unexplained mysteries, and folklore.

When Shawn had told her to choose the location of their trip, he had hoped she'd pick something along the Long Trail, which was maintained and easy to get one's bearings on using a glossy guidebook or even one of the old, photocopied trail maps Shawn had collected over the years.

But no. Of course, that would be too easy.

Instead, Gracelyn had scoured books, websites, and articles looking for weird events and supposed fantastical beasts in New England. She had a lot of these for her blog. She'd tossed around ideas of chasing Bigfoot on remote trails in Maine, searching for Wild Man—a Bigfoot-like creature—in New York. Or what did Shawn think about

looking for Pukwudgie or the Beast of Truro in Mass-
achusetts? Shawn had merely smiled and shaken his head.

"Let's stay in Vermont, Gracie. We're only going to have a
long weekend. Don't want to waste it on the road."

In the end, she'd chosen Diablo Point.

Shawn supposed he should have felt relieved. The
mountain was practically in their own backyard after all.
But he'd felt uneasy instead. He'd grown up with the stories.
Didn't think that Bigfoot was real or that tiny versions of
men like the Pukwudgie actually existed. But the snake...was
different. Shawn doubted it was as big as some accounts
made it out to be, he didn't relish the thought of coming
face-to-face with anything larger than a garter snake. He
hated snakes and had since he was a kid. But he couldn't
very well tell Gracelyn that he was too scared.

"Come on, Dad," Gracie had wheedled, reading the look
on his face. "My readers really want to see Diablo Point up
close and personal. It'll be great, right?"

He'd nodded his head stiffy, making assuring noises and
asking questions about what, if any, camping gear his
daughter would need. But underneath his flannel shirt, his
heart pounded hard.

Emily had told him he was being foolish. That night
when they'd crawled beneath the freezing sheets in their
drafty bedroom in the old farmhouse, she'd snuggled close
to him.

"You shouldn't let her have her way all the time, Shawn,"
she'd said, then breathed a yawn into his shoulder. "There
are a million places you could hike. Why go up there?"

Because Gracelyn wanted to, he almost responded but
then caught himself. He'd been listening to different
versions of, "you spoil that girl," and "she has you wrapped

around her little finger," more times than he liked to think about.

And yes, she did sometimes go too far, act too selfishly. But there was another side to Gracelyn that he loved so much it hurt. The part of her that cried when they showed those homeless and abused pets on the TV commercials. The fire in her that had blasted bullies on the playground who picked on smaller kids. The acidic tongue that got her into trouble with school officials, but also spoke the truth when other people spouted sweet sticky lies.

He loved her honesty and her fiery-ness, her headstrong attitude and her devil-may-care approach to life. She wasn't irresponsible. She didn't become an alcoholic in high school or have a baby when she was fourteen or do drugs, at least not that Shawn knew about. She was just...spirited. And curious. Gracelyn had a quick, inquisitive mind that needed to constantly be fed new things—new ideas, new information, new possibilities—in order for it to function right. For her to function right.

And the fact that she was legally blind had nothing to do with it. He told himself for the hundredth time. She could do this trip on her own. She'd hiked an impressive number of peaks both in and out of New England solo. She'd had a guide dog for many years—Trek—and climbed a number of those mountains with him by her side. But he was gone after an aggressive form of cancer. After he'd passed, Gracie had sworn off dogs.

Shawn paused and looked around him. He forgot sometimes how beautiful it was out here. His work as an electrician kept him busy and mostly indoors. He still walked every day, no matter the weather. But this was different. It felt sacred out in the stillness. Cares and worries and stress unwound themselves slowly and slid down your body until they pooled in the mountain dirt under your boots.

"Come on, slowpoke," Gracelyn called back. Shawn could barely see her above him on the trail. Silhouetted in the early morning light she looked to him both more fragile and stronger than she ever had before. He smiled and quickened his pace.

3

GRACELYN EDWARDS

DIABLO POINT TRAIL

Present Day

"Do you think it was worse to lose your vision or to have never had it, to begin with?" Gracelyn wondered how many times she'd been asked that question over the years. She didn't have an answer. Had it been tragic losing her vision as a teenager? Yes. Would it have been worse to have never seen anything since birth? Likely.

Being legally blind was different than full blindness where you're in total darkness all the time. Gracelyn had worked hard over the years to explain this to friends, teachers, even her family at times. She needed to remind them too, that she wanted to focus on what she could do independently, not what she couldn't. Because she could see shapes, colors, movement—could even read street signs if the lighting was right—and could read things like maps or even books if she used a powerful magnifying glass or if the text was greatly enlarged.

Still, it was challenging explaining her situation and what she could and couldn't see to an employer or a potential new friend. How could she tell them that so much of it depended on the quality of light, the situation she was in and even her own fatigue? When she was fresh and alert, Gracelyn could see best. When she was tired and depleted her vision decreased.

Most people who met her didn't realize she was legally blind until they either spotted her sweeping her walking stick in front of her—she'd refused to use a traditional white cane—or overheard her audible map.

Juvenile macular degeneration was the official medical diagnosis. But to Gracelyn that had always felt like little more than a scratchy label, a too-tight box. And if there was anything she was good at, it was bursting out of constricting boxes.

Gracelyn had scaled peaks—alone—in both the Green and the White Mountains. She'd traveled to Montana for a single week of white water rafting with friends and had fallen in love with both the water and a river guide named Mack.

Mack.

Gracelyn frowned and stirred the hot enamel cup of instant soup. The steam coated her mouth and nose as she blew on it. Thinking of him brought their last conversation to mind. It felt like months had passed since then.

"I'm going with you, Gracelyn," he'd said, his forehead sporting a deep line between his brows. His light brown curls partially hid it and part of her had wanted to put a hand there, push the curls back and smooth away the line, the frustration.

Instead, she'd clenched her fists.

"It's not an option." The words were quiet but sounded hollow to her own ears.

"I know what you're planning, what you think you're going to do. It's incredibly foolish."

She'd snorted. "Yeah. Roger already told me that. Did he tell you?"

Ignoring the question, Mack asked, "Then why won't you listen?" His voice turned pleading. Gracelyn felt something inside of her quake. He'd looked at her, his face almost clear in the bright morning light.

She'd just shaken her head. "I have to do this."

He'd exhaled loudly through his nose, shaken his head.

"You don't. Do you think this is what your father would want?"

His words ripped at her heart like the barbed ends of a whip.

"Gracelyn," he'd moved closer, put a warm, calloused hand over her arm. "Please rethink this. If not for yourself, than for your family. For me."

She'd smiled but shrugged away his hand. She couldn't —wouldn't—let Mack or Roger decide this for her. She knew herself. This was something that she had to do or she'd never find peace.

The sudden screech of a bird startled Gracelyn, nearly causing her to spill her soup. She lowered the cup to the ground and sat back against the stone. She didn't feel hungry anymore. She had the same uncomfortable sensation that someone was watching her. She glanced around, scanning the forest but not seeing anyone or anything out of the ordinary. A branch snapped on the other side of the trail and Gracelyn turned. The sun was directly overhead now and the forest was as illuminated as it would ever be for her.

Green leaves danced overhead in blurry blocks of color. Sunlight poured through the branches and felt hot on her skin. A bead of sweat trickled down her neck and she itched at it distractedly.

There was a rustling sound coming from the trees. Gracelyn stood slowly, her left hand going automatically to her backpack. She didn't move her eyes from the spot of the noise. It was probably an overeager chipmunk or squirrel, but she wasn't taking chances.

She felt the cool barrel of the Ruger under her fingertips and moved them along until the rough grip fit into her palm. More rustling. Then silence for a few seconds. The rest of the forest was filled with noises suddenly, making it harder to hear. Two birds argued overhead. Tree branches to her left squeaked together and as the wind moved in the forest, it breathed through the pine boughs, making it sound like people murmuring quietly.

Then two branches snapped in quick succession. Gracelyn lifted the handgun in a single fluid motion and pointed it toward the noise. She couldn't see anything. She squinted, tried to make out any shapes moving.

There was nothing.

Seconds later a fat, gray rabbit hopped out of the under-growth. Gracelyn laughed weakly and released her arm.

"Better be careful, bunny," she said as she returned the gun to her bag and sat again by the fire. "Or you'll magically turn into someone's stew."

The bunny turned and plowed through a clump of ferns near the trail.

Gracelyn picked up her cup of soup and took a sip. The hot, salty liquid tasted good. She pulled a chunk of bread from the bag near her feet and dipped it in, relishing both the smell and flavor.

She ate her fill, then sighed in contentment. For a few minutes, Gracelyn would forget about why she'd come on this trip and what she planned to do and just enjoy the woods.

4

SHAWN EDWARDS

DIABLO POINT TRAIL

Two Years Ago

"Did anyone talk about it when you were growing up, Dad?"

Shawn glanced over the fire at Gracelyn, the stick in his hands in mid-break. He was snapping them into smaller pieces and feeding them into the crackling campfire in front of them. They'd finished a delicious meal—made over the little Jetboil camp stove—and with a full belly and several miles on his legs, Shawn was sleepy. He snapped the stick and tossed both pieces into the fire.

"Sure, they talked about it. The Settlement has been here for ages. Kids used to dare each other to go into the remaining buildings."

"Did you ever go in?" Gracelyn's eyes were wide, searching through the low light to find his face.

"Ayup. Had to do it to impress your mom."

"Really?" Gracelyn's voice held that note of excitement it always did when she was learning something new. "What happened?"

Shawn chuckled. "It was a long time ago, kiddo."

"Come on."

He covered a yawn somewhat successfully and rested his head in his hands behind him, leaning onto the large boulder.

"Well, let's see. I've told you before that your mother was the prettiest girl in our entire school."

Gracelyn groaned. "There were like twenty kids in your school."

"Not true. There were close to a hundred, just twenty in my graduating class. Anyway, when your mom moved here, I thought I'd died and gone right up to heaven. She was not only gorgeous but also worldly."

"She'd moved here from Brattleboro."

"I know that. But it's a big city compared to Bondville. Anyway, she was the most sophisticated girl in school. One afternoon a group of us was walking home. We were probably, oh, I don't know—ninth grade? Maybe tenth?—and Richie Jones dared one of us boys to go into the old Sutter house with him. I volunteered."

"Were you scared?"

Shawn laughed. "Ayup. But I'd seen your mother's face when Richie had suggested it. She looked as terrified as I felt, so I knew I had to do it."

"What was it like?"

"Old. Broken down. Sad mostly. There was a spooky feeling to it but I don't know if it was because the old place was really haunted like the kids used to say or because I was scared out of my wits. Anyway, Richie and me poked around in it a little. Dared each other to go upstairs which we did. A lot of the floor was rotting away up there. There were holes in the roof and God knows what kind of animals were living in it. We saw nests in the corners of a couple of rooms and the whole place stank of bat guano. Phew," Shawn shook his head, letting his arms drop. "That's a smell you don't forget."

"What else did you see?"

Shawn paused, thinking back. A huge hole, big enough for him to crawl through that looked like it had been punched in the door to the basement. He still remembered the jagged edges and the way the wood had buckled outward. It had been made from the inside, someone—or something—had wanted very much to get out of that cellar. But Shawn didn't tell Gracelyn this, or about the line of rusted locks that marched down the door.

"Not much. We tried going down into the basement but couldn't get the door open," he said mildly. "Richie said it was because the family was still under there, that their souls were holding the door shut. But I'm pretty sure it was because the floor was all buckled from moisture.

"Anyway, the place was a death trap. It might have been one of the houses that have fallen in now. A few sort of imploded during summer storms or from the weight of the snow over the years."

"Did you go into any of the other buildings?"

"Just the mill. I used to play there with Pete when we were kids."

"Gram didn't mind?"

Shawn grinned. "She didn't know. She was working in town then and we had free run of the countryside pretty much after chores were done. We didn't start helping with haying and driving the tractor and stuff till we were a little older."

"Well, how old were you when you and Pete played in the old mill?"

"I dunno. Seven? Maybe eight?"

"You were that young and out by yourselves?"

Shawn nodded. "Things were different then. I was in charge of Pete and being a year younger, he followed me wherever I went. I didn't think much of it at the time but it was dangerous in retrospect."

"Must be I get it from you," Gracelyn said.

"What's that?"

"My taste for adventure and danger."

Shawn threw his head back and laughed. "Yeah, must be."

They were both quiet for a few minutes, staring into the fire. Shawn glanced up, the sky overhead stopping his breath in his chest. It was beautiful. The clouds they'd seen earlier had dissipated. Pinpoints of light a trillion miles away were spread across the velvety indigo sky like someone had tossed glitter everywhere. Lighter shades of blue framed the darker, making the entire sky look alive.

He looked back to the fire, shot a glance at Gracelyn out of the corner of his eye. The light illuminated the planes of her face, smoothing them. She seemed to glow. She was a beautiful girl, though not in the traditional sense. Her nose was too long to be classically beautiful, but like Emily, she was striking. Gracelyn's eyes, ironically, were her best feature. They were large and framed with long, dusky-colored lashes. Shawn looked back at the fire and shifted against the boulder.

"We should turn in soon. Want to get an early start tomorrow morning."

"Sure," Gracelyn said, but made no move to stir. Shawn didn't either. The fire was hypnotizing.

His thoughts returned to The Settlement—that's what the residents of Bondville had dubbed it—and the hole in the basement door. That day with Richie, Shawn had been the first to spot the tracks in the dust and grime, along the floorboards. Not footprints, not paw prints. More like the tracks his bicycle tires made. Only thicker. Much, much thicker.

They'd stopped right near the top of the basement door. Right outside the gaping, yawning hole in the wood.

"It's where the snake comes in and out," Richie had breathed close to Shawn's ear. His breath had been hot and smelled like leftover tuna fish and the yellow lemon candies he liked to suck on.

Everyone in Bondville back then knew about the snake. It was supposed to be huge—bigger than any other snake on earth—and it was said that it guarded The Settlement. Other people told a different story: that the snake had once guarded the town and had then gotten loose, killing every inhabitant. Now, of course, there were few left in the town where Shawn had grown up and fewer still of those who had heard the legend of the snake and believed it.

But that hot, dusty summer afternoon, Shawn had felt his heartbeat rapid-fire in his chest. He'd stared at the hole, expecting any moment to see a set of glittering eyes or a forked tongue in the darkness. He hadn't seen either, but something had made those thick, winding tracks.

Richie had shoved him toward the closed basement door and Shawn had jumped, startled by the motion.

"Ha! Gotcha," Richie had said. Then, "Come on. Let's get back. This place is boring." All of Richie's "s" sounds hissed due to two missing front teeth. Pond hockey was Richie's favorite winter activity.

Shawn had turned to follow him, relieved to be leaving

the close air in the smelly house. But as he'd turned to go, he could have sworn he'd seen something move on the other side of that hole. He'd blinked and looked again. There was nothing there. Other than the line of rusted locks and open hole. Shawn had left the old house.

5

GRACELYN EDWARDS

DIABLO POINT TRAIL

Present Day

Gracelyn stumbled over a tree root, cursed and leaned momentarily against a tree. The poplar's smooth bark was welcome under her shoulder as she leaned into it, let its weight support her. The light was fading. Already the afternoon sun was waning, its rays weak. The woods around her were thrown into shadow.

In the mountains, the light came later in the morning and was blocked out earlier in the evening. But still. She'd planned to make it to Hidden Lake in Buzzard's Gulch for the night. She needed to refill her water bottles and the relatively flat ground around the lake, sheltered by the steep stone walls, would provide a good, solid place to set up camp.

How far away was she? Gracelyn peered at the map again in the light but it looked smudged and dirty. Sighing, she pulled the heavy pack from her shoulders and propped it against her shins. She dug through the supplies till her hand found the plastic bag storing the flashlight, headlamp, matches, fire starter and other supplies that would be affected by moisture...or an unexpected fall into a brook. She removed the flashlight and magnifying glass, shone the light onto the map.

It didn't give her the good news she'd been hoping for. Her fingers traced the route between where she believed she was to Hidden Lake. She groaned. Could she really be that slow? The last time she'd hiked here with her father—

Images flooded her mind at the thought. Like someone laying out a stack of glossy photographs in front of her: Dad, laughing at something she'd said, his eyes bunching up around the corners; the sound of his low, deep voice as comforting as it had been in childhood; the sound of his feet treading the path behind her...and then other pictures. His face frozen in surprise. His mouth gaping open. His eyes—

No.

Gracelyn chewed her lip and traced the line again with her fingertip. A glance up toward the sky told her there was maybe another hour of daylight at most. She missed Trek acutely at that moment. Like a physical appendage, the seeing-eye dog had been part of her for years. But Trek was gone. Dad was gone. She was here though and making it to the lake tonight, no matter what.

Stuffing everything back into her bag, Gracelyn kept out the battered headlamp and tucked an extra battery into her pants pocket. Then she repacked the bag, cinched the top tightly and pulled it over her shoulders. They throbbed and groaned. She ignored the discomfort, grabbed her walking stick and started upwards again.

This part of the trail was less densely overgrown due to the higher elevation. But it was steeper—much steeper—

than what she'd hiked earlier. There were more loose stones too, easy to catch with one's foot or roll an ankle. She wasn't sure but imagined that the stones slid down the summit during storms. The top of Diablo Point was covered in shale and other gray rocks that Gracelyn didn't know the names of.

The air was sweet though and she focused on the aromatic blend of pine and moss and ferns and the loamy scent of decaying leaves underfoot. One foot in front of the other. *Step, step, step, step.* Rather than leaning on the walking stick she now used it more to guide her, sweeping it outward in front of her, low to the ground. It clanked against a stone on the side of the path, smacked against a small tree, warned her of downed logs nearby and occasionally, the slippery runaway rocks.

Close to an hour later, Gracelyn smelled the water. She smiled, used her stick and the headlight set on its brightest setting to pick a trail downwards into Buzzard's Gulch and toward Hidden Lake. The abrupt change, from steep incline to descent was disorienting. She took her time, feeling her way with the stick and her hands at times, to make sure she wouldn't fall.

Gracelyn grinned when at last her feet hit the broken shale that made up a narrow beach. Above her, she could feel the looming presence of the steep cliff face. It surrounded the lake on three sides. The fourth was flanked by the woods that dropped off steeply.

It was called a lake but was actually more of a quarry, albeit one made by nature. No one knew how it had been formed and its location in this remote place kept it from being discovered by anyone but the most avid hikers. People in Bondville didn't talk about it with outsiders. And unless you grew up here, chances were good you wouldn't know about it. The hikers Gracelyn had seen earlier were the exception. She hadn't asked but would bet that one or both of them had relatives in Bondville or had lived there once.

Gracelyn let her backpack slide to the ground. Then she followed the sound of stone underfoot to the water's edge. It was deep—incredibly deep—and black. A bottomless pit. The water was said to be home to all manner of amphibians and reptiles. Gracelyn could never work out how much of that was the truth.

Stories made up a huge part of the town. It was endearing at best, frustrating at worst. Gracelyn figured, if one lived in Bondville, one was prone to tall tales. The never-ending winters and the messy mud season that followed bred stories of fantastical creatures, many of which were variations on other regional folk legends.

But what about the snake? a little voice inside asked. *That wasn't just a story, was it?*

Gracelyn shrugged the thought away and blamed the goosebumps on the cooler air. She needed to set up camp, she thought. First, though, she walked to the lake, knelt and ran her fingers through the cold water. Gracelyn clutched the filtered water bottle in her hand and plunged it into the water. She capped the bottle and brought it to her lips, droplets of water running from her hand down her chin. The water was fresh and delicious and she drank deeply. When she'd finished, she refilled the bottle and then did the same with a second one.

Returning to her pack, Gracelyn moved slowly in the near-black. It had just past dusk, so a seeing person would still be able to see without the aid of artificial light. But her world had already turned dim, except for the faint illumination cast by the headlamp.

The forest around her had grown quiet, a lull before the

nighttime sounds began. Gracelyn hastily erected her tent under a small grove of overhanging tree branches away from the lake. There was less shale here and though it wouldn't be a comfortable night's sleep, at least she wouldn't have stones digging into her through her sleeping bag. There was also less chance for an animal to spook her, coming to get a drink in the middle of the night.

Too tired to make a fire or even fire up the camp stove, Gracelyn nibbled on a granola bar. She'd need to get the bear bag with the rest of the food high up into a tree before she fell asleep. She yawned and turned out the headlight, relishing the darkness for a moment. It engulfed her completely. Now, other than a far-away dim slice of moon, she couldn't see anything. Her eyelids grew heavy and she slipped into a light sleep.

The rustle of some nighttime animal—a skunk maybe or raccoon—in the undergrowth near the thin strip of beach, woke her. She lay on the ground in her tent and tried to get her bearings. How long had she been asleep?

Breathing deeply, Gracelyn unzipped the tent. A fragrant mix of earth and the dusty smell of hot stone and a slightly fishy smell from the cold lake greeted her. She flicked the headlight back on, setting it on full strength. She drank more water and ate an apple, tucking the core in with her uneaten food when she'd finished. Then, Gracelyn cinched the bear bag. It wouldn't be easy to try to get it over a tree branch in the dark but she'd made a mental note of a good branch several yards from camp. Ideally, it would be further away, but she'd work with what was available.

Getting the bear bag into a tree was a slow and frustrating process. It required hooking rope—weighted by a stone—over the branch of the tree. This involved throwing the stone repeatedly, trying to lob it over the branch. Once she'd done it, she'd scurry over and grab the rock, pulling the bag up high. Lastly, the rope had to be knotted on itself to prevent the bag and everything else from crashing back to the ground. Sometimes a particularly determined animal like a raccoon got to the food anyway. But other than hauling along a bear-proof box or going without eating this was the only viable option.

Gracelyn's arm was sore and her shoulder throbbing when she finally got the bag up near the branch. She made the knot, pulling it tight to make sure it wouldn't loosen, then retraced her steps to camp and sank gratefully down onto a stone outside the tent. Her heart was thumping hard in her chest. She tilted her head back, let it rest on the hard boulder. Was it the same boulder Dad had leaned against that night? Regret rose like a wave inside her.

If only...

If only they'd never come. If only there had been a storm and they'd gone home early. If only she'd chosen somewhere else—anywhere else. If only...She tried square breathing again but kept seeing her father's face. She listened to the noises around her, tried to distract herself by identifying every one of them with her eyes shut. Nearby, a branch snapped, then another and a third. Something large was moving through the undergrowth. Gracelyn shoved her feet back into her boots, laces loose and fumbled for her pack. It was beside her where she'd left it.

Where was the noise coming from? She listened closer. The left. Back near where she'd come out of the woods and onto the narrow strip of rock littering the edges of the lake. Just beyond the site of her tent.

The gun. Where was the gun? She swiveled, plunged her hands into the pack that was still gaping open. She felt around for the familiar rough handgrip.

More branches cracked and then she heard the sound of feet moving over stone. The air was oppressive with humidity and fear. It clung to her skin like a physical thing.

She looked toward the place the noises were coming from. Her headlamp—even at full power—didn't illuminate a body, human or otherwise. She heard her breath, a quiet panting as she squinted, tried to make out shapes in the black void before her.

Nothing.

Everything around Gracelyn fell away. She focused all her attention on the exit of the trail.

She squinted hard.

Something moved.

A couple of saplings undulated. There was the sound of more twigs and branches snapping. Then she saw a dark figure, human, emerge from the overgrowth.

6

SHAWN EDWARDS

DIABLO POINT TRAIL

Two Years Ago

Morning had dawned but it was hard to tell. A heavy fog had rolled in overnight and engulfed the mountain.

"It'll burn off with the sun," Gracelyn said over a breakfast of quick oats and trail mix. But it didn't. They'd gotten a later start than they'd intended after discovering a water bottle had come uncapped and soaked through most of Shawn's pack. He'd dried things off the best he could and they'd finally started upward. They were on the steepest part of the trail now. Rather than becoming clearer the further they ascended, the thick mist pressed down on them. Shawn's skin was coated in moisture and his clothes were damp and heavy.

Gracelyn had resorted to using her walking stick like a cane, tapping out the trail in front of her. He followed her boots around another bend, then bumped into her when she stopped abruptly on the path.

"There it is," she breathed, her voice a quiet whisper. She had a monoscope, an extra-high powered one that was meant for birdwatchers and was squinting through it. Shawn followed her pointing finger, as white as bone in the dim midday light. Shawn squinted. The rock outcropping they stood on provided a good look at the peak. Or would have, if it hadn't been covered in rolling fog. Shawn grabbed his own binoculars for a better look.

He could see the craggy mountaintop, covered in stone. Only a few of the hardiest trees dared to make their home on the ledges and even these were bent and crooked. The wind must tear at them during every storm, try to pull them from the ground. He scanned the area with the lenses but saw little else other than the shale and layers of loose stone on the ground.

"See it? Back down to about two o'clock from the top," Gracelyn said, peering through the monoscope. She looked like a pirate. Shawn smiled and trained his binoculars lower. The smile slipped from his face. A gaping hole was cut into the side of the mountain. He pulled the binoculars away from his face. The hole was still there, inky black against the gray stone. He replaced the lenses to his face. His breath stuttered in his chest and he swallowed, trying not to let his fear show.

Gracelyn knew her father didn't like snakes, but she didn't know the extent of Shawn's fear. And he wanted to keep it that way. There had been another time exploring The Settlement that he hadn't told her about. A time when Pete had saved him, running for help after Shawn had fallen down an old shaft at the mill. They'd been playing cops and robbers—Pete, as always was the cop—and the day had been perfect. Puffy cotton ball clouds in a robin's egg blue sky. The trees had felt almost alive—green leaves shiny and dancing in the breeze. Shawn had closed his eyes at one point, smelling the faint odor of woodsmoke and the tang of some flower he couldn't name nearby.

"I'm gonna get you!" Pete had crowed, running out from behind a big tree, his little battered toy pistol aimed at Shawn.

"Oh no you ain't," Shawn had yelled back and taken off at a dead run. He'd glanced back over his shoulder in mock horror—Pete loved it when he really got into the game—and heard something crack loudly. It took his brain a minute to realize that the sound had come from underneath him. Like ice on the lake, the hidden, rotting wood beneath his feet split open and swallowed him.

The shaft had been dry, thankfully. Shawn had been too frightened to scream as he fell, his hands scrambling to find something—anything—to grab on the way down. He'd hit the ground hard, blue lines wiggling and dancing before his eyes. And then he'd blacked out.

When he'd come to, he'd seen Pete's face far above him. It was red and snotty and his little brother's hair was mussed. He'd shouted when Shawn opened his eyes.

"You're alive!" he'd yelled. Then, "I'm gonna get help!"

Shawn had moved his head slowly from one side to the other. He'd tested his legs and arms, his fingers and toes. Everything hurt but all of it moved which he assumed was a good sign. His head throbbed hard and when he put a hand to the back of it, he felt warm stickiness. Still, if he'd split his scalp it wasn't the worst thing in the world.

He'd frowned. His mother would not be pleased to learn they'd been playing here. She'd forbidden it the last time Pete had slipped and said something about a ghost in one of the houses in The Settlement. Maybe Pete would find Mr. Stanger. The quiet farmer likely wouldn't mention it to their mother.

The old shaft was cold and damp and smelled strongly of dirt and worms. Shawn wished he had a light to shine around. It had taken a moment or two for his eyes to adjust enough to see that he wasn't in the space alone. First one, then another slithering body darted in the shadows. As Shawn stared, frozen in place, he realized that he'd fallen into the home to a nest of wriggling, writhing snakes. *They're not poisonous. They're not poisonous.* He kept telling himself that over and over as he held in screams of terror.

One crawled up into his pant leg and he jumped up, head woozy and slapped at his corduroys until the snake fell back out. Seconds later, another dropped onto his shoulders. Shawn had lunged to the side of the well, twisting and writhing himself until he flung it loose. The feel of the snakes' cool, dry skin, the muscle of their bodies twisting over him. He shuddered, remembering the panic he'd felt that day. The despair as he'd dizzily clawed at the walls had tried to scale them. And how he'd slid and fallen down again and again...

He shut his eyes now.

"...I think."

Gracelyn had said something. Shawn shoved away the image of the snakes, the smell and the pressing closeness of the earth and tried to focus.

"Say again?" His voice was surprisingly normal sounding.

"I said it should be only another forty-five minutes or so to the cave. I think." She turned, glanced at him. "Don't you?"

Shawn took his time replacing the lens covers on the

binoculars and slipping them back into his pack. "Ayup," he said finally. "Seems about right. An hour at the most."

"Dad." Gracelyn moved closer, put a hand on his arm. He was surprised. She wasn't a touchy-feely person. "It's going to be great. We'll just climb into the cavern, snap a few pictures for my blog and then hike up to the top, just to say we did it. Easy. We've got this."

He smiled at Gracelyn. Jerked his head toward the trail. "We'd better get going then. Maybe we can make it back to Hidden Lake for a late lunch."

His stomach twisted at the thought of food and beneath his canvas pants, his knees trembled. It was the exertion he told himself. Just overtired muscles.

Gracelyn grinned and put away her scope, before snatching up her walking stick and plunging upward on the trail.

THE OPENING in the face of the mountain was not easy to get to, even for a person with normal vision. There were tricky handholds and the sliding shale underfoot made each step slippery. Still, Gracelyn had insisted on going first. For once, Shawn hadn't bothered arguing with her.

Now, they stood in the dimly lit entrance of what amounted to a hole. It wasn't big enough to be called a cave and was so narrow that they were bent over nearly double. Shawn leaned against the wall, brushing spiderwebs away from his face and trying not to gag at the smell. Whatever lived here ate meat. The foul smell of rotting flesh emanated from somewhere further down.

Once, a little mouse had died in their living room. For weeks whenever Emily or the kids would walk into that part of the living room, they'd nearly gag from the smell. They'd looked everywhere—under the entertainment center, behind the old wingback chairs and coffee table—trying to find the cause. It was only months later after the odor had faded completely, that they'd found its little skeleton frame in a wall while replacing an outlet cover.

The tunnel smelled like that, only a thousand times stronger, and the tightly enclosed space made it worse.

"Need help?" Shawn asked.

Gracelyn had dropped her pack and was rummaging through it. "No," she whispered. "I just have to find my other camera. It does better in dim lighting."

Why hadn't she thought of it before now? Shawn wanted to ask. His skin felt itchy and he couldn't stop scanning the dark space, imagining a thousand snakes pouring out of the tunnel-like a scene in *Indiana Jones* or something

Come on, Gracelyn. Come on, come on.

"Got it!" she said holding a shiny metal thing overhead. She left the rest of her pack undone, clothes and tools spread around on the tunnel's floor and fiddled with the camera.

"I put it on the right setting already because I figured it would be too hard to see in here," she whispered. "I'm just going to snap a few pics and then—"

A noise sounded from the back of the tunnel. Rocks falling? It sounded like it to Shawn. He glanced at Gracelyn. Her eyes were wide in the dim light but it wasn't fear on her face. It was excitement. The noise came again, like a few stones tumbling down from someplace higher up. There was a gentle clink, clink, clink and then a louder clunk, maybe as the rock hit against others on the bottom of the tunnel's floor.

"Hurry, Gracie," Shawn said his voice an octave higher

than usual. "Whatever is back there, we don't want to run into it in its home."

Gracelyn didn't answer but did start snapping pictures. "I set the aperture high and am using a really high shutter speed," Gracelyn said. Her voice was higher than usual too, but she was smiling and biting her lip at the same time. "Both should help in the low light. It was a little tricky to get the settings right but I hope—"

Another sound filled the space. At first, Shawn thought it was running water. It hissed and rolled forward in the dead air, coming from somewhere far back in the tunnel. Coming toward them.

He imagined what might make a noise like that. Things that actually made sense, not fairytales about giant snakes. But all Shawn could picture were the tracks in the dirt at the house in The Settlement. And the jagged hole in the basement door. The door with the row of rusted locks lining its edge. What could have made those marks on the floor? What were the villagers keeping in the basement?

You know what, said a little voice deep in his brain.

"Gracie, we've got to go," he said. He leaned over and picked up her bag, started stuffing everything in willy-nilly.

"Okay," she said, but took two steps forward. "Just a couple more shots. Wouldn't it be incredible if I got an actual photo of—"

Her words ended in a scream. Shawn bolted upright out of his crouch, the pack falling from frozen fingers. He stared. A head appeared in the tunnel before them. It was serpentine and wide. So wide that Shawn blinked twice, three times, sure he was seeing things that weren't possible. But it was still there. And set on either side of the massive head were two very bright, very shiny eyes.

Eyes that looked directly at Shawn and Gracelyn.

7

GRACELYN EDWARDS

DIABLO POINT TRAIL

Present Day

Gracelyn watched as the figure moved against the darkness of the trees on the outskirts of the pebbled beach.

"Hello?" a voice called.

Her hand clutched the gun's grip. She hesitated, then pulled it from her bag and hid her hand behind her leg. A faint light bobbed, near the end of the trail. The beam of a flashlight. She remembered suddenly the pair of hikers she'd met earlier. Her hand loosened slightly on the gun. Other people—however infrequently—did use this trail.

Still.

"Hello," the voice called again. Then, "Gracelyn?"

But this voice was familiar. She knew it as well as her own. Her palms were clammy as she hurriedly replaced the gun. Her eyes scanned the area where the light bobbed. She still couldn't make out anything other than a little glow of white and a human shape.

"Mack," she said, her voice hard. "Why did you come here?"

Mack's calloused hand stretched over his face to block out the high-intensity light of her headlamp.

She flipped the light upward.

"Geesh," he muttered. "If you gave me a warmer welcome I might ignite in flames."

There was a pause. This was where Gracelyn was expected to say, "I'm sorry". She didn't.

"I can't believe you," she said instead. "I cannot believe that you did this, Mack. I told you that I was fine, I didn't need any help."

"Yeah, you've told me that in many ways over the past year, Gracelyn," Mack said. He was the only one in her immediate circle that didn't call her Gracie. Even that annoyed her at the moment.

"So why did you?"

"Man, do we really have to get into this right now? Can't I at least get my tent set up and—"

"What? No. You're not setting your tent up here. I've already claimed the only good spot."

"Well, if that's an invitation to share—" Mack's voice told her he was smiling.

"It's not."

He half sighed, half laughed. "I was kidding, Gracelyn. And there's plenty of room for two tents, maybe even more if the neighbors didn't mind being friendly."

"Well, I do mind. I'm not feeling especially friendly."

Mack snorted and she knew he was grinning. This made her even madder.

"Look, Gracelyn—" he started but she cut him off.

"No. Listen to me. I. Don't. Want. Your. Help. Do you understand that? I didn't ask you to come here and I don't want you here."

"Yeah, got that message. Loud and clear. The thing is whether you want me here or not, I'm here. This is a free country. This land isn't your personal property. So, I'm staying. And I'm setting up camp. Here."

"Fine!" she yelled, her voice cutting through the quiet. "Suit yourself. But I'm leaving at first light and don't you follow me."

"Don't worry, I won't," Mack said. She heard his feet moving over the broken shale, further down the beach toward her left. "I'll be up at the top waiting for you."

"Don't you dare!" she snapped and threw her bag, half-opened into her tent forcefully. She was surprised not to hear a plop as it blew out the back of the tent and landed in the lake.

"Just leave me alone. That's all I've ever wanted."

Mack snickered. "Ever? I think you're exaggerating, Gracelyn. There was a time when you wanted me around. I remember it really well. You can't tell me you don't." His voice had changed, dropped an octave. Gracelyn wished he was standing in front of her again so she could punch him.

"Oh, shut up."

Mack whistled cheerfully and moved off to the left to set up his camp. She heard the normal sounds of someone making camp: the zip of the tent, and the nylon-on-nylon sound of the sleeping bag and maybe a pack sliding against the tent's fabric. Gracelyn sat unmoving in her own tent, still not quite believing he'd followed her up here.

Later, she heard the pop and snap of a fire and could see the glow through the pale blue walls of her tent. She lay, fully clothed on the floor. Sharp stones poked at her back and jabbed her ribs. Gracelyn didn't care and she didn't move.

Smells of something salty and hot cooking made her mouth water.

"Mmm, nothing better than chili over an open campfire," Mack said. "And I even brought a couple of Hostess fruit pies. I happen to know those were your favorite. Are they still, Gracelyn?"

She didn't respond.

"Let's see, what flavors do I have here?"

Mack rustled around in his pack.

"Oh yeah. Man, I got both blueberry and apple. Is apple still your favorite?" He went on when she remained silent. "I'm prepared to sacrifice and share it with you. Along with some hot coffee laced with a little of the old bourbon—"

"I'm sleeping," she yelled. Blood pounded in her ears. Part of her realized she was being stupid and incredibly childish. A bigger part of her didn't care.

How dare he do this to her? They'd talked it over. He'd told her that what she planned to do was too dangerous to attempt on her own. That hadn't gone over well. She smiled now, remembering his contrition in the end. Of course, it was clear that Mack hadn't been giving in at all. Heat stained her cheeks again. He'd just been lying, making her believe he would respect her wishes. But he hadn't.

Gracelyn rolled into a sitting position. What was she doing? Acting like an idiot, that's what. If she calmed down, spoke with Mack rationally, he would see her point of view. Then he'd give her the space to do what she needed to do. Alone. And afterward, they could go their own separate ways. It would be better that way.

Gracelyn straightened her clothes and ran her fingers

through her hair. Calm. Cool. Collected. She repeated the words over and over like a mantra as she set out her bedroll and sleeping bag, tucked the backpack in the corner of her tent and unzipped the tent's narrow nylon door. She would go and speak with Mack like a normal, civilized person. He would see things from her perspective and everything would be fine.

~

"I HATE YOU." Gracelyn moaned the words the next morning on the trail. The air was already hot and thick. Her mouth was still pasty and dry, even after brushing her teeth and drinking what felt like a gallon of fresh water.

"No you don't," Mack said from behind her. "You love me deep down."

"Well, it must be very, very deep," she replied. "Because I certainly can't feel it."

"Doesn't matter, it's there," Mack said and started whistling.

"Shhh," Gracelyn hissed over her shoulder. She stopped so suddenly Mack bumped into her. "Not only is my head about to implode but do you really want to give our location away?"

"Sorry," Mack said, his voice serious. "No more whistling. Or talking."

"Good," Gracelyn mumbled.

They'd spent more than two hours talking by the fire last night. Gracelyn had eaten not just one but two Hostess pies and washed them down with Mack's bitter, bourbon-laced coffee. They'd talked finally—really talked like they hadn't in weeks—and she'd convinced him that this was something she had to do on her own. He'd nodded, agreeing whole-heartedly. And then they'd shared a little more bourbon minus the coffee. He'd tried to help her back to her tent eventually, but she'd flailed at him and stumbled there herself.

But it had been Mack who'd helped her up when she'd tripped over a fallen log and sprawled on the stony beach.

"Lightweight," he teased as he opened the zippered door for her. The sound of the metal teeth had made Gracelyn laugh.

She'd turned to him in the pitch black, her hand automatically going to his face. It was rough and smooth and familiar under her fingers.

"Mack, I have to tell you something," she'd said. "I—"

"Don't, Gracelyn. Not now," he'd held his own hand against hers for a moment before squeezing it and letting it go. "Tell me in the morning if you still remember what it was."

He'd dropped a kiss on her head like she was his kid sister and backed out of the tent.

Gracelyn frowned now, her cheeks hot. She was thankful at least that she hadn't told him what she'd planned to. Then her embarrassment would be overwhelming. Bad enough she'd drunk too much and let her guard down. And why, she wondered not for the first time that day, hadn't he tried to follow her into her tent and sleeping bag? She frowned, unsure if it made her respect him or feel insulted.

"There it is," Mack's voice cut through her thoughts. Gracelyn followed his finger to the side of the mountain just ahead of them. The light was good today and there was no fog like the last time she'd been here.

"You sure you still want to do this?" he asked.

The black, gaping hole opened wide like a jagged mouth cut into the side of the mountain.

Slowly, Gracelyn nodded. "Yes," she whispered, "I have to."

8

SHAWN EDWARDS

DIABLO POINT TRAIL

Two Years Ago

"Run," Shawn hissed close behind his daughter. She was frozen to the spot, staring straight ahead. He wondered what she could see in the dim light. Gracelyn stumbled backward a step. Her boot caught on a loose stone. The snake didn't move.

"Gracie?" Shawn's voice was a harsh whisper in the oppressive space.

"I—" Gracelyn took another step backward, then another. Shawn gripped her upper arms as soon as she was close enough to reach. He put his body between her and the snake, guided her backward while glancing over his shoulder toward the snake. His pack. He needed to get into it. The gun was right up on top of everything else. He'd been impatient with Gracelyn for not having the camera ready. How stupid was he to not have the gun in hand, or at least tucked into his waistband?

Almost there. Shawn could see the opening before them
—ten feet? Fifteen at most—and caught a whiff of fresh air.
Suddenly, a sound behind him. Rock on rock. Stones
clinked together loudly.

Gracelyn screamed.

Shawn pushed her toward the opening and whipped
back around. The snake loomed over him. It was close. So
much closer than Shawn could have thought possible. Its
big, muscular body rotated slowly, from one side to the
other. It had skimmed over the stones almost silently. Its
strange eyes watched them, and then its tongue—my God it
was long—flicked out. It nearly caught the edge of Shawn's
jacket.

"Go," he yelled to Gracelyn. "Get out of here!"

"No!" she screamed. "I won't leave you."

The snake looked from Gracelyn to Shawn. Back again.
Its dark eyes glittered. Then it slowly started to raise itself
up. Up, up in the too-narrow space, its head touched the
tunnel's ceiling, its enormous body filled the earthen cavern.
It was darkly colored and had some sort of pattern on its
scales. Shawn couldn't do anything but stare at first. He
looked and looked, trying to get his brain to accept what he
was seeing.

The snake had a perfectly triangular head and it flicked
its tongue out, sampled the air. The tongue was black. And
as it pulled its lips back slightly, Shawn saw rows and rows
of serrated white teeth.

Finally, he moved. Shawn slipped the pack from his
shoulders and thrust a shaking hand inside. He had to get
the gun. *The gun. The gun!*

The snake looked sharply toward Shawn's hand. Its tail
whipped out from behind its body and flicked toward him.
Then everything seemed to move in slow motion. Shawn

noticed how strange the tail looked: a pale, pale pink and thin, almost like an earthworm had gotten stuck on the big snake's body. The rest of its tail higher up was normal: dark and scaled, but funneled down into this strange, worm-like appendage at the tip. Gracelyn yelled something. It didn't register with Shawn.

At first, he didn't feel anything, other than the dry, hot feeling of the tip of the snake's tail passing over his leg. Then an incredible burning heat. Next, a dull warmth stole over him. Like Novocain at the dentist. Only now, Shawn's entire body started to grow numb. He glanced down, trying to make his hand grip the gun's stock. Instead, it lay by his side. His side? How had it gotten from his pack to his side? He didn't remember doing that.

Shawn heard Gracelyn scream. It sounded like she was underwater. With an effort that seemed mammoth, Shawn formed the words: "Run, Gracie." They came out slow and garbled like he had a mouth full of marbles and was talking around them.

His leg burned where the worm-like tail had struck it. Shawn looked at his pants and saw a small round red circle through the khaki material. Was that blood? His shins and knees were thick and heavy like big weights had been attached to them. He stumbled, tried to catch himself on the wall closest to him. It was damp and greasy under his hands like dishwater left too long in the sink. The numbness crept upward. His torso now, his belly all tight and thick feeling. It was like he was turning into the Michelin Man, Shawn thought. It made him want to laugh but now his chest and neck and cheeks were frozen too.

Had Gracie gotten away? He tried to turn his head but couldn't. He listened but could only hear the sound of the stones hitting each other as the snake came closer and closer. It had a peculiar smell. Like a mix between burned toast and decay. A loud droning sound filled the air but Shawn couldn't tell if it was in his head or filled the tunnel itself.

"Get out of here!" Gracelyn yelled. A big rock flew through the air from the entrance of the tunnel and bounced ineffectively off the wall of the cave. She was throwing rocks at it.

Run, Shawn yelled, but the words wouldn't come out. The snake jerked, looking from Shawn toward the tunnel's entrance. Toward Gracelyn. It slithered in that direction, its thick body winding over the rocks in an "s" shape.

"Run, Gracie. Please run," Shawn said. But the words were stuck in his head. His mouth wouldn't move. His breath had begun to change too, coming in jerky, short gasps. He tried to stop it, tried to slow it down, but couldn't.

Shawn felt himself fall then, sideways like a tree felled in the forest. He remembered watching his dad help his uncle cut trees sometimes on his farm. Shawn had liked the crash as it fell and then the boom as it hit the ground. But he hadn't liked the way it looked afterward, the gaping hole in the sky and the splintered, jagged trunk poking up from the ground.

Laying motionless on his side, Shawn heard Gracelyn's feet skittering near the entrance of the cave. Then a loud crack. She'd lobbed another stone inside. The sound of feet over stones. Then a single gasping scream.

Then nothing at all.

Shawn lay there, helpless, trying and failing to move part of him, any part at all. *Move, move!* he shouted at his useless limbs. His brain was the only thing that seemed to be working but even it felt slowed down and dull. It took him several long moments to realize that the snake had returned after Gracelyn's last panicked cry. He tried to twist his head, see the serpent but couldn't. Instead, he stared straight ahead at the wall of the tunnel. Hair-like roots poked out of the walls and thicker ones twisted around themselves and the earth. He saw something yellowish caught in one of the roots. It was rounded, but not perfectly. A ball? The snake slithered closer. He could smell it before he could see it. The snake moved off toward the deeper part of the tunnel. It was a skull, Shawn realized as he stared at the yellowish ball. A human skull caught in the roots.

There was a tugging at his ankles. Then Shawn felt himself dragged over the stones. It didn't hurt. The smell of decay grew thicker the further back the snake pulled him. Shawn's lolling head caught sight of the snake in front of him, weaving its way back toward its lair. It faced toward the back of the tunnel, its tail wrapped firmly around Shawn's legs. It was strange: the way that the snake now kept the worm-like part away from Shawn's body. Shawn flicked his eyes forward but it was too dark to see where they were going. Heartbeat slowing. So cold. The venom. Numbing everything.

The darkness around him pressed down like a physical weight. He tried and failed to blink. His eyes were closed. He couldn't open them. Before the darkness stole over him completely, Shawn's last thought was, *please, please let Gracie make it.*

GRACELYN WOKE with her heart pounding. Her throat was dry. At first, she didn't know where she was. There were trees above her standing listlessly in the heat. Bugs screeched in the hot air.

The trees around her spun crazily and Gracelyn tried to sit up and collapsed back onto the ground. She lay on her side, panting and waiting for the dizziness to pass.

The next time she tried to sit upright, she propped herself up gently on a nearby boulder. Her arms were covered in scratches from the fall. Her hands were wrapped tightly around something hard. Gracelyn closed her eyes again and moaned. Her head throbbed and one spot felt especially tender. She focused her line of vision on a point far in front of her and managed to slow her breathing down. The white light of the sun helped Gracelyn to see things around her more clearly.

Slowly, slowly she pushed herself up on the boulder, first sliding her butt up until she was sitting, then carefully rising to a standing position, using a nearby sapling to stabilize herself. She'd fallen—out of the tunnel and then down the slope—and somehow, miraculously, managed to not kill herself in the process. The hard thing in her hands, she was amazed to discover, was the camera. The one she'd used in the tunnel to take pictures of—

Her brain sputtered to life.

She had to go get help.

"Dad?" She called, but her voice was little more than a ripple in the heat. She was about to call out again but stopped herself. The snake didn't know she was still alive. If it didn't know then it would leave her alone. She could get down the mountain. Go get help. The state police. A search and rescue team. The FBI. There had to be people who would help her. Help her father.

Gracelyn choked down a sob, tried to get her bearings. Assess the situation: she'd blacked out when she'd fallen. But she remembered the moments before. She'd thrown a stone into the tunnel and missed the snake, but another one had hit it, close to its eye. Then it had lunged toward her. She'd stepped too far back and had fallen. She shivered now, remembering it. The feeling of nothingness behind her. The empty space where there should have been ground underfoot.

She'd been desperate to grab anything that would hold her. Her hands and arms had connected with some sort of prickly, scraggly bush and she'd latched onto it like a drowning person. But then watched in horror as the bush fell away and her hands, greasy with sweat, lost their purchase. Then she'd been falling, falling for what felt like a very long time.

She remembered hitting the ground hard. So hard, it felt as if the earth beneath her sucked all the air out of her body. She had laid there staring up at the leaves. Then the world had turned black. Nothing had hurt when she'd first come to. But now everything did. Mostly her arms and her head which felt as though someone was repeatedly thumping an axe into her skull.

Gracelyn put the camera carefully into her pocket and took a few more shaky breaths. She had to find the trail. If she got lost, couldn't find it...well, they would both be in a lot of trouble. This forest was thick and remote. And she didn't have anything she needed to help her. The special compass and map and magnifying glass, her whistle, and cellphone, even without reception, were all in her pack in the tunnel.

The thought of the space made her gag reflexively. And her father—

No.

She couldn't. Not now. She'd end up a mess of tears and snot and that wouldn't do Dad any good. Her body didn't cooperate though and a single sob erupted from her throat. She choked back another.

Stop it. Stop. Panicking is the worst thing you can do. Dad needs you. You're his only hope.

Gracelyn swallowed hard, reached down and pulled a long, thin branch from the forest floor. It was too long, so she snapped it in two. Flailing it out ahead of her, she used it as a cane. She hit low branches and climbed painfully over them. The makeshift cane smacked into stones and boulders which she skirted. She could see well enough without it, in this bright light. But this made her faster. And faster was better, especially now.

Many minutes later, Gracelyn found the path. The tangling undergrowth gave way to the trail which in comparison, was relatively smooth. She looked back up toward Diablo Point. It was further away than she'd imagined. That was good. She was making good time.

"I'll be back soon, Dad," she said out loud. "I'll get help. I promise."

9

MACK COOLEY

DIABLO POINT TRAIL

Present Day

The Green Mountain National Forest runs across the southwestern and central parts of the state and covers more than 400,000 acres of land. Peppered with rugged peaks and stunning views the area is home to animals like black bears, bobcats, fox, a large variety of birds, rabbits, and other herbivores. Mack had read up on it before starting out on the Diablo Point Trail. While Gracelyn had grown up in this area, he wasn't as familiar with the geography. When he'd pictured it, he'd always imagined Norman Rockwell paintings and good skiing.

The forest map Mack had picked up showed different regions intended for a variety of purposes: recreational areas, backwoods areas, alpine ski areas, diverse forest use areas and one called simply, "wilderness". It was in this area that Diablo Point Trail was located. It wasn't recognized or maintained by the government, which is why the trail was severely neglected. As often happened in rural states, there simply weren't enough resources to go around.

He'd read up on Diablo Point, too, though the history of the peak was slim. He'd learned that past generations had made their own trail, using the mountain as a shortcut to another town, one that would have taken days of travel by road. Mack couldn't imagine living here, in a place this rural. Gracelyn had told him that much of the National Forest was bordered by small towns. Some so small they weren't recognized as towns at all.

Mack stretched his neck from side to side, trying to work out a kink he'd gotten while sleeping on the hard, stone-covered ground. Gracelyn had told him that the small settle-ment of Bondville had been handed down through the generations; like Grandma's unwanted china. Children were shuttled to a nearby three-room country school by parents. Buses didn't travel that far out. There weren't many families anyway and what few there were shrank on an annual basis. Young people moved away and old people died.

Unlike the mountains out West—Mack had done a lot of climbing in the Rockies and the Pacific Northwest—the Green Mountains were more like large hills. But mountain ranges shouldn't be judged by elevation alone.

Whereas the western mountains were craggy and tall, New England's were hard and unforgiving. Some lacked switchbacks, those gentler approaches to ascending and descending that hikers appreciated. Here, Mack often found himself on trails that were so steep he had to use both hands to haul himself up. In other places, resourceful hikers had built ladders over rock faces and stone or wooden steps right into the mountains. Sheer drop-offs were not unusual. The small signs warning of the danger were easily overlooked: covered with tangled undergrowth, thick bunches of dried leaves or in winter, he imagined, snow.

Now though, he worried more about needing a blood transfusion. Mack swatted at another mosquito as he followed Gracelyn up the trail. The bloodsuckers were thick. The humidity of the forest and little muddy pools in low depressions along the trail a perfect breeding ground. It had been a wet summer and hot too.

A mosquito flew up his nose and he snorted.

"What?" Gracelyn called back. "Did you say something?"

"Nope. Mosquito," he said.

"Oh."

They fell into silence again. Gracelyn used to joke that she was built for the woods, not just because of her fitness level but also because of her thick skin. She was convinced the people either had thick or thin skin—literally—and that was why bugs left her alone. Her skin, she reasoned, was thicker than the average person's.

Mack wasn't so lucky. If Gracelyn's theory was true then he was on the thinner-skinned spectrum. Biting insects loved him.

"It's because you're just so sweet," Gracelyn had joked that summer they'd gone rafting. Back when she used to joke.

Mack rubbed a hand over the back of his neck. It came away damp and with two smushed insect bodies on it.

"Should be there in a few more minutes," Gracelyn whispered loudly.

"Okay," Mack said but his stomach clenched.

He'd put on a good show for Gracelyn, but the truth was this whole thing terrified him. That was if he thought about it. So, he chose not to. Instead, he distracted himself with memories of the summer he and Gracelyn had met. He'd been a guide out in Montana then. She and a group of her friends were taking one of the white water rafting tours he and another guy, Jason, had been leading. Mack had bribed Jason with a six-pack to swap groups when Gracelyn had climbed into the other raft. Jason had laughed and shaken his head but switched boats.

Gracelyn did an impressive job not only on the water—keeping her cool when several of the other newbies shrieked and/or fell overboard—but hiding her blindness. In fact, when her friend mentioned it casually that night around the campfire, Mack assumed she was joking. The friend, seeing his disbelief had smiled.

"Don't tell her I told you," the dark-haired girl had said. "She'd kill me."

After he'd gotten to know Gracelyn better, he understood the warning. Her temper flared easily and often, but only if you tried to get her to do something she didn't want to. Or implied that she couldn't do something. Even a hint of protectiveness would earn you the sting of her sarcasm accompanied by a smile.

Yet underneath all of that, Mack had sensed a vulnerability. Maybe he'd fooled himself. Maybe he'd been looking for something—some traits—that weren't really there. But he'd convinced himself that if she let him in, Mack would find a deep, old pain in her core. He could sense it. The same way that he could tell if a barking dog was really going to bite or was just putting on a show.

And he'd been right. After they'd spent hours and hours together—first on the trails and rivers in Montana, then the high bluffs of Wyoming—Gracelyn had finally opened up. About her father and how much she missed him. It had taken a year but finally, she'd broken down one night and cried. It was the first and only time she'd done so. She'd sobbed soundlessly. The shaking of her shoulders and the dampness on his shirt the only sign that she'd been crying. It was soon after that that Mack had convinced her to come back. To face whatever it was she'd been running from. He'd told her that he'd be right there with her.

And he had. Until their argument. They rarely fought but in this case, "argument" made the exchange sound too civil. There had been breaking glass, a hole in the wall, words screamed in frustration and anger. But he'd expected Gracelyn to calm down afterward. To come around. To see his logic.

She hadn't done any of those things.

Instead, she'd plowed ahead with her plans as bull-headed and frustratingly stubborn as always. Mack wanted to stay mad at her, but couldn't. Maybe, if she hadn't let him in before. If he hadn't seen that scared little girl part of her, the one who felt so guilty about what had happened to her father...maybe then—

"Stop for a drink?" Gracelyn asked.

"Sure."

She stopped and grabbed for the water bottle secured to the side of her pack. Her chest was heaving slightly and her face damp with sweat. Her blonde hair curled around her cheeks in tiny, spontaneous ringlets. It surprised him, seeing her sweaty and out of breath. This hike was more of a technical challenge than a physical one. Still, Gracelyn hadn't been pushing herself hard since they'd come to Vermont. Instead, she'd drifted into a depressed fugue state.

"Doing all right?" Mack asked. When he saw her eyes narrow in his direction he wished he hadn't.

"Fine," was all she said. It was a word in a sentence. Period. The end.

He gulped some water and looked up at the mountain's

peak. It was getting closer. Though the trees were dense in the woods, they were becoming shorter now, closer to the top. And the canopy overhead was growing thinner too. Light poured in with fewer leaves to block it out. Nearby a couple of birds squabbled over something.

"Gracelyn," he paused. He needed to say this in just the right way or they'd be back to square one. "Remember my friend, Ron?"

"Mmm," Gracelyn responded and took another swig from her bottle.

"He worked on that state road crew, taking care of the rockslide down south of your mom's place?"

Gracelyn nodded.

"Well, when I knew I'd be coming with you I asked him for a favor. It was a pretty big one, but he owed me some money...long story. It involved a poker game."

Gracelyn smiled. "Why am I not surprised?"

Mack kept going. She wasn't going to like what he had to say.

"The thing is...I got some, uh, supplies from Ron to help us. To help you, I mean. For when we get up in the tunnel."

"Supplies?"

"Yeah." Mack took a drink from his bottle and then continued as nonchalantly as possible. "He hooked me up with some explosives."

The silence was so loud it hurt his ears. Gracelyn's mouth was partially opened, whether from pleased surprise or dismay, he wasn't sure.

"Are you serious? I cannot believe you did that."

Well.

Mack had his answer.

10

GRACELYN EDWARDS

DIABLO POINT TRAIL

Two Years Ago

Hours later, Gracelyn made it to the spot where she and her father had camped the night before. She pushed on. If she kept going at this pace, she could make it back to the car by early the next morning. Maybe. It would be hard. Especially after night fell. In the dark, it would be challenging even for a seeing person to make it in these woods, on the overgrown trail. After the sun went down her vision would quickly grow worse. From blurry to a small pinprick of light at best and that was with a strong headlamp or flashlight. Without either? It would be like running down the mountain in pitch darkness. Still, she wasn't going to sit around and wait to be rescued or take the time to set up camp for the night. Not when Dad was still up there. Not when that thing had him.

It had done something to her father, paralyzed him. She'd never heard of a snake having venom in its tail like a scorpion. But then, she'd never heard of a fourteen-foot serpent either.

She thought about Hidden Lake, made her brain focus on it and tried not to picture her father around the blackened circle of ash that they'd left the night before. But it didn't work.

When she closed her eyes and leaned momentarily against a big tree, an image of him appeared. And then more pictures of him marched across her mind in unison: Dad racing her up the highest part of Mount Mansfield; his eyes crinkling in the corners like ginger cookies after she'd bagged her first solo peak in New Hampshire; Dad picking her up off her feet and swinging her around in a giant bear hug when she'd come back from her first summer job, working for a fishing company in Maine.

He'd always supported her. Always. Where her mother didn't understand her—or chose not to—Dad had always gotten her. Or at least pretended he had. Gracelyn pushed away from the tree. Trips down memory lane weren't going to help Dad. And neither was taking a break.

The woods were quieter today. An occasional flapping of wings overhead or distant call of a bird were the only sounds. Even the trees had stopped their graceful dancing. The leaves hung in a limp canopy as though even they were too tired and overheated to move. The air was hot and heavy, like a damp beach towel. Cicadas whined periodically, the only thing breaking the quiet.

Gracelyn continued downward. Her heart was pounding, her feet nearly flying over the trail. Every step, she swung the walking stick out in front of her, correcting her footing when it tapped against a rock or limb or root. As she ran, she planned. If she made it back by midnight the authorities would start an immediate search. They had to, didn't they? Every state was different, of course. It depended on where one needed rescuing as to how the situation would be handled and how quickly. Gracelyn couldn't remember what the rules were here. Well, She'd make sure that this search started immediately. Hold on, Dad. Hold on. She used the words to mark the progress of her feet. *Hold on, Dad* right-left-right. *Hold on*, left-right.

Hold on, Dad. Hold on. Hold on, Dad. Hold—

Gracelyn's right foot caught on something—a log? A branch?—and she sprawled forward onto the low-lying undergrowth. Her hands scraped against a big stone half-buried in the ground. The breath whooshed out of her. She lay there for a second, assessed the damage. She was all right. She had to be all right.

She pushed up onto her hands and knees and cried out. The sound was like a gunshot in the quiet woods. Her ankle. Oh God, it hurt. Was it caught in something or?... She looked back but couldn't make it out with her blurred vision. She moved into a sitting position. Or tried to.

A burning arc of blue pain ran through her ankle. She gasped, then leaned forward on the cool earth with her palms, trying to redistribute her weight.

Stupid. Stupid. Stupid. How could she have been so care-less? Hot, pulsing pain throbbed in the ankle. Was it broken? Maybe she'd just rolled it. Gracelyn maneuvered herself into a sitting position, dropping down onto her left thigh and buttock. Slowly, using both hands, she guided her right leg forward. Now both legs were in front of her. The foot was already swelling; she could feel it throbbing painfully in her boot.

Stupid!

Gracelyn shook her head, tried to clear it. Lambasting herself wasn't going to make the situation any better. Tentatively, she turned the foot to the right. The same mind-exploding blue pain shot through her and she gasped.

Okay. Likely broken. So, what should she do?

She'd need a splint. A couple of straight branches. Rope from her pack. The first aid kit for painkillers. Then she remembered: her pack was still up in the cave.

It took several frustrating minutes to stand up. A wave of dizziness engulfed her when she first righted herself, so she leaned on a nearby tree and swayed until it passed. Then, hopping and using her walking stick, Gracelyn moved into the woods far enough to find a long, fairly straight branch. The problem was that in order to break it, she needed both feet: one to jump on the branch held at an angle against the ground, the other to stand on. She'd have to improvise.

Gracelyn pulled the branch behind her to a fallen log. The downed tree had been there a while, the bark soft and flaky under her hands. Moss had sprouted over the area where it had broken from its stump. She placed the branch against the log, wedged it between the stump and the ground as hard as she could. Her scraped palms didn't like this but she ignored them. Then she pressed down on one end of the branch. The first time it slipped out of her hands. She stumbled forward, barely catching herself on the big downed tree before she fell flat onto the forest floor.

She tried again. The second time the branch started to slip from its spot between the stump and the earth. She jammed it in harder, then counted to three and pushed as hard as she could on the upper part of the branch, wobbling on her one foot. It rewarded her with a loud crack and split neatly into two.

Gracelyn repeated the process again to get two smaller size branches. Then she hopped back to the trail. She fumbled with her bracelet, one she'd had for years. It was made of paracord and when it was unwound, she'd be able to use the rope to bind her ankle. Stretching her leg out in front of her again, Gracelyn pressed her lips together. This would not be pleasant.

First, she had to remove her boot. The foot inside was so swollen it promised to be a painful process. After that, she'd create the splint, lashing it tightly enough to provide support, but not so tightly that it would cut off the blood supply.

A film of sweat had broken out over Gracelyn's forehead. Whether it was from the heat and humidity or plain fear, she wasn't sure. Ignoring the feeling and the sweat, she loosened the laces of her boot. Her fingers were shaking and it took her two tries to get the knot undone. After that, Gracelyn took a big, deep breath. Without waiting, she eased her foot from the boot.

The leaves around her whirled wildly as the dizziness hit her again. She bit her lip to keep from crying out. Because of the ninety-degree angle of her rigid boot, she couldn't just slip her foot easily out like she would with a sneaker or slip-on shoe. The high wall of support that the boot offered meant that she had to turn her foot, angle it upward in order to then get her heel and the rest of her foot free.

Grimacing, Gracelyn stuck her fingers down the back of the boot and used them to leverage her heel out, slowly guiding it up the boot's high sides until finally, her foot was out. Her foot was puffy and the skin around her ankle had expanded out over the top of her sock. It looked pink and when she put a hand over it, the skin was hot. Pressing her lips together, Gracelyn lined up the branches. She frowned. She needed padding between the branches and her skin. She ripped the sleeves from her shirt and wound the fabric loosely over her lower leg and ankle. Then she wound the paracord over the entire thing, making the knots snug but not too tight.

When she'd finished, she sat back against a nearby tree and let her breathing return to normal. The dizziness was fading and the nausea was gone. She was incredibly thirsty and wished she had her pack with her. Ibuprofen, water, food, her compass, and map—everything was in that pack.

She groaned and rolled onto her knees, grimacing as her right ankle twisted slightly with the motion. Using the walking stick and the tree she'd been leaning on, Gracelyn maneuvered into a standing position. She felt victorious to be upright again, ankle hurting but immobilized. It would be easier to descend with crutches but Gracelyn didn't have the time or energy to attempt making a pair.

It was going to be a long, uncomfortable night on the mountain.

11

MACK COOLEY

DIABLO POINT TRAIL

Present Day

"I cannot believe you have explosives with you. Right here. Right now." Streaks of hot pink ran from Gracelyn's neck into her cheeks.

"They used it for a job they finished up a couple of weeks ago. I told Ron what we needed and," Mack shrugged. "And he offered to help out."

Gracelyn slapped a hand to her forehead. "Do you know how incredibly stupid that is? You could blow us both up if you fell. Or if your backpack is jostled—"

"No, it's not like that. TNT is actually really stable. I read up on it and—"

Gracelyn snorted. "Mack."

"Would you just hear me out? I wouldn't do anything to put us in danger. And I wouldn't just stuff it in my pack, not knowing what the repercussions are. You know me," he lowered his voice an octave. "Do you seriously think I'd risk our lives like that?"

She was silent a moment. Then, "No," she said her voice still exasperated. "But—"

"Have I ever done anything risky just for the sake of it?"

"No," she said more softly.

"In all the time you've known me have I ever once put you in danger? Or been reckless or careless?"

She was silent for a long moment. "Well. Not unless you count the time you played chicken with the eighteen-wheeler in Wyoming—"

He didn't realize she was joking at first.

"Haha," he said. But a smile pulled at his lips.

"You almost peed your pants that night," she said.

"What about you?" he asked. "I believe I heard something like, 'oh God, I don't wanna die in this stupid car.'"

She chuckled. "Well, it was a pretty crappy rental. Remember the cigarette burns on the ceiling? And that smell—like wet dog."

Mack nodded.

"Anyway, it's still fun to see you squirm. From time to time." Her smile deepened. She had two dimples that made Mack crazy. He hadn't seen them much in the past several weeks.

She sighed. "So, what. Ron just asked his boss for a few extra what—bricks? Packages of TNT?—and walked off the job with it tucked in his lunchbox?"

Mack took another swig of water and shook his head. "No. Ron's in charge. Or at least the second in command of that little unit of guys. His boss is more a behind-the-desk type, tired and about to retire. He doesn't get out of the office any more than necessary. So, Ron takes care of the day-to-day." Mack paused to wipe his mouth with the back of his hand. "I didn't ask him details. I just asked if he could help and he said he could. It's only a little anyway. Enough to do what we need to. I also have a drill to bore the hole and the detonator. Don't worry, Gracelyn. You can trust me."

"I brought two guns, Mack. I think I'll be able to take care of the snake with that."

He shrugged. "Just think of this as a backup."

She lifted her eyebrows. "It seems pretty invasive. I mean, explosions can't be good for the mountain."

"No," he said. "But it might save our lives...not to mention other people who find themselves up here. Anyway, chances are we won't need it. You'll go in there, guns blazing and do what needs to be done. I just wanted you to know that there's a Plan B. If you do need it."

She was quiet a moment, then replaced her water bottle. "Well. Thanks, I guess."

He nodded.

They hiked on. The undergrowth became sparser the further up on the trail they went. Now the old path was easier to make out. Physically it was more challenging, though because the terrain became steeper. Mack heard his own breathing deepen. His calf muscles had started to ache, a feeling he enjoyed.

About twenty minutes later, they'd arrived at the final climb. Here, the trail split into two directions, right and left. To the right a barely visible trail swept over the side of the mountain, passing by the ominous black hole Gracelyn had pointed out. The snake's tunnel was that way. To the left, a path went straight up to the pinnacle. That path was more worn than the one to the right.

"I think the snake made it," Gracelyn said as she looked at the trail leading to the tunnel. "That trail—" she stopped.

"Listen," her voice had dropped to a whisper. "Do you hear that?"

Mack listened but didn't hear anything other than the normal sounds in the woods and their breathing in the nearly still air.

"What?" he finally asked. "I don't hear anything."

"I think it's moving around in there."

He didn't have to ask what "it" was or what "there" Gracelyn was talking about.

"Already? I thought we'd have more time to get—"

Gracelyn held her hand up in the universal stop gesture. Mack listened harder. Her ears were better than his—better than most people's—because she'd learned to depend on them more than her vision. She closed her eyes now, to listen harder he guessed.

"It's moving," she said moments later and opened her eyes. "Hopefully it will stay in the tunnel and we'll be able to sneak in without it knowing we're even there."

He followed Gracelyn's bobbing backpack as it turned to the right, toward the tunnel up over their heads. The greenery here was mostly nonexistent, though a few trees—bent over nearly in half from the wind—were rooted on the sides of the mountain. Scraggly bunches of thorn bushes hung tenaciously to the side of the rocky peak.

Mack could see now what Gracelyn had meant about the rock. Underfoot the dirt of the trail was replaced with chunks of shale in all different sizes. It was slippery and noisy underfoot.

Gracelyn stopped suddenly and Mack bumped into her.

"Sorry," he mumbled.

"I have a new Plan A," she said. "We're going to go in the backdoor."

"Is there one?"

"I don't know. But we'll find out. It'll be better that way. There's no chance of us surprising it and sneaking in through the front, not with the racket we're making." She kicked a foot at the rocks underfoot.

Mack nodded.

Gracelyn changed course, leading them back to the "v" where the trail had split.

"Chances are good there will be an exit somewhere," she mumbled over her shoulder. He could see her using the walking stick more frequently now, tapping it and tracing it in long arcs over the ground. He wanted to tell her to just let him go first, let him lead and help her over the occasional debris but he knew better.

"Right," was all Mack said.

They followed the path to the left up to the summit. The view was uninspiring, offering only a glimpse of more, larger mountains nearby and little else. The peak was also dangerous. The slippery shale underfoot slid constantly, making it dicey to stop moving. Gracelyn's solution appeared to be not pausing. Instead, she led the way over the top of the mountain, circumventing the summit by several yards and immediately heading down the back side. Here, the terrain was different, more hospitable. The shale turned back into larger rocks and dirt, making it easier to get around. It was still steep though. In several places, the ground just dropped away.

"Mind if I lead for a bit?" Mack asked, prepared to be turned down.

Gracelyn paused. "Yeah. That might be a good idea."

Mack didn't wait for her to change her mind. He hurried in front of her. There was no trail here. Instead, he used the mountain's summit as a marker.

"What are we looking for exactly? A hole like the one on the other side?"

Gracelyn made a noise that sounded affirmative.

Okay. Mack kept his gaze moving between the higher points above them that were too steep to walk on and the trail he was bushwhacking. There was more vegetation on this side of the mountain. It must be more protected from the wind.

They made their way slowly around the mountain. Mack didn't see anything. No hole. No gap in the craggy surface. Nothing.

They kept going.

The sun was hot on his skin. He glanced up at it. It was past noon, probably closer to two o'clock. He grimaced. Even if they did find another way into the tunnel now, how would they do what they needed to and get out of the woods before dark? Maybe they could at least make it back to Hidden Lake. It hadn't been such a bad place to sleep. He'd certainly had worse camping spots—

Mack stopped in his tracks. Above them, under a little overhang was something dark and jagged cut into the terrain. It was a hole. A gaping mouth in the side of the mountain tucked well under the stone overhang.

"Gracelyn," he said, his voice low. "I think we've found your exit tunnel."

12

GRACELYN EDWARDS

MEDFORD POLICE STATION

Two Years Ago

"And so you're saying that this...." the voice faded before turning into a cough. "This giant snake grabbed your father?" Officer Jakes asked again.

Gracelyn let her forehead drop into her hands. She'd been through the gamut of emotions since arriving at the station: hope, fear, anger, frustration, incredulity and now despair. It had been risky telling the truth. But she'd wanted the men and women who made up the Search and Rescue party to be prepared. It didn't seem right sending them up Diablo Peak without knowing what they were facing.

She groaned and cupped her hands over her eyes, staring straight down at the laminate-top desk under her elbows.

"Yes. For the eighteenth time. Yes, there is a huge snake living in that mountain. Aren't you from around here? Haven't you heard of the—"

"Gracelyn," her mother said, her voice full of apology.

The sound only made Gracelyn angrier.

"It's in a tunnel. Near the top. My father and I went into the tunnel. I showed you the photos—"

"With all due respect, ma'am, the pictures are so dark that you can barely make out the walls of the tunnel. I saw no evidence of any animal, serpentine or not, in any of them."

"Well, I didn't get a photo of the thing while it was lunging toward us, okay? I was a little preoccupied trying to get out of there before it ate me—"

Her mother spoke up again. "Gracie, please." Her voice broke and Gracelyn could feel her arm move beside her, hear her mother sniff as she dabbed at her face with another damp tissue.

"What are the next steps?" her mother asked the officer across the desk. Gracelyn heard the squeak of his chair as he leaned back in it. He was blurry but her mind filled in the gaps: thinning hair, pale eyes, indistinct features, and a beer belly that he rested his clasped hands over now.

"Well, we just have to wait. Search and Rescue is combing the area. If your husband is out there, they'll find him. Of course, whether or not he's been, er, accosted by a giant snake, well..." His voice trailed off again. Gracelyn wanted to reach across the desk, grab a handful of his shirt and smash his face into the desk.

"Whatever happened up there, I just want Shawn back safe," Gracelyn's mother said. "Is there anything at all we can do in the meantime? Any way we can help?"

"No, ma'am, I can't think of anything." His chair squeaked again. Gracelyn let her hands drop. She sank back into the hard straight back of the chair she was sitting in. The room around her was dimly lit and made it hard to see the details of the things in it. She could see the desk in front of her, of course, blurred around the edges. There were some file cabinets against the back wall. Other than that things looked fuzzy. It was a cramped office in a small police station two towns over, and it smelled of old coffee and stale BO. Gracelyn wasn't sure if it came from the officer or previous visitors.

"Well, now there is something," Officer Jakes said. "Maybe you could go over to Town Hall—it's just down the street a block away—and help with the refreshments. They're setting up some food and drinks for the Search and Rescue team, for when they get back. I'm sure they'd appreciate an extra set of hands."

"Of course," Mom said.

"Just one set, Officer Jakes?" Gracelyn's voice was loud in the small space. "I think I can handle making sandwiches. I'm not an invalid."

"No. No, I didn't mean—"

"Whatever."

"Gracelyn." Her mother's voice was sharp.

Gracelyn got up from the uncomfortable chair. Her legs were still shaking from overexertion, her ankle—treated as soon as she'd found help back in town—was stiff and swollen in the elastic bandage wrapped tightly around it. It had been a sprain after all, not a break. She grabbed for the crutches her mother insisted Gracelyn use and hauled herself toward the door. The *thump-thump-thump* of the rubber tips grated on her nerves.

"Thank you for all your help," Gracelyn's mother said as Gracelyn fumbled for the door handle. "I appreciate it. And I'm sorry about..."

Gracelyn didn't stay to hear the rest. She was halfway down the hallway, feeling her way every few feet by trailing her fingers over the chair rail before her mother caught up with her.

"There's no need to be so rude," Mom said. Gracelyn could sense her mother's anger under the usually calm surface. "He's just trying to help."

"How? By not believing me? And insinuating that I can't do something simple like make sandwiches because I'm blind and worthless."

"That's not what he said—"

"No, but it's what he meant, Mom."

Her mother half-laughed, half-sighed. "Gracie, when are you going to stop this?"

"Stop what?" Gracelyn paused in her angry march down the hall, feeling her mother's fingers grip her forearm.

"Stop being so angry at the world? Stop acting like a...a spoiled brat when things don't go your way?" She stopped a moment, as though weighing her next words.

"Do you know that your father is terrified of snakes? Absolutely hates them. But he went on this trip with you because he loves you and couldn't say no to you. And now you're being rude to the very people who are trying to help us find him—"

"Officer Jakes didn't believe me, Mom! I'm telling you—there is a giant snake up there in the mountain. I'm not making up stories. It grabbed Dad. It pulled him back into the tunnel. I know what I saw—"

"Stop. Please." Her mother's hand fell away. "I've heard enough about giant snakes and Bigfoot and pigmen and little hairy people living in the forest to last me a lifetime. Those aren't real. They're just folktales. They're not real," she repeated.

"Mom, I—"

"Enough." Her mother's voice was clipped around the

edge. "I am going to find Town Hall and see what I can do to help. It would be nice if you did the same. There are people out there risking their lives for our family. I think it's the least we can do."

Heat climbed up Gracelyn's cheeks but she didn't say anything. Just waited until her mother's footsteps retreated. She heard the front door open with a squeak and then the footsteps disappeared.

It was quiet in the police station. In fact, Officer Jakes was the only one on duty it seemed. It was almost six o'clock in the morning and the air blowing in from the door that had just opened was soft and sweet compared to the stale interior of the station.

Gracelyn wanted to scream and pound her hands against the walls of the stupid police station. She wanted to go back to the little smelly, cramped office and demand that the officer believe her story. That he recognize she was not a liar, nor a stupid, helpless girl. She wanted to chase down her mother and shake her and tell her that she was wrong. That her father went with Gracelyn because he loved adventure, craved it just the way she did. That he'd wanted to take this trip as much as she had.

She didn't do any of those things. Instead, she hopped down the stairs on her good foot. She threw the crutches behind a thick hedge bordering the police station and started walking. Her ankle hurt but the high dose of painkillers was doing its work.

Gracelyn knew where she needed to be and it wasn't at Town Hall stuffing egg and tuna salad into bread.

Her father was out there.

He needed her.

∾

"THANKS," Gracelyn said as she climbed out of the car. It had been too cold with the air conditioning turned up on high. She shivered as she stood by the side of the road, waiting for the car to drive away. It didn't.

"Are you sure your friends are meeting you here?" the man in the car asked. His voice was high and reedy. "I can wait with you if you want."

"No, thanks. They'll be here in just a few minutes. I appreciate the ride."

A pause. Then, "Well, if you're sure." His voice was uncertain.

"I'm sure," Gracelyn said. She knew his type. Needed absolution of the potential danger he was putting a blind girl into. That way if something happened to her, he could swear—truthfully—that he had hesitated at leaving her alone in the forest. That'd he'd offered help but she'd turned him down.

The car moved off down the dirt road, its tires crunching and popping over loose stones. Gracelyn could feel and taste the hot earth in the air, rising from the ground in a swirl as the car drove away.

The engine noise faded. The forest was quiet in its wake. Birds chattered overhead and further away, Gracelyn could hear the noise of a different engine. It sounded big and growly. Maybe a truck run by the Search and Rescue team. It could be their mobile headquarters.

She'd purposefully asked the driver to let her out at a trailhead further down the mountain. She didn't want anyone on the search team to see her, to stop her. Reaching down, she felt around in the undergrowth until she found a good walking stick. Then she crossed the road and checked the signs at the trailhead. They were blurry but if she leaned in close she could just make out the words, Knife's Edge.

This trail connected further up with Diablo Point, she was pretty sure. Of course, since Diablo Point wasn't marked on a map and wasn't open to the public, she wouldn't see that information on the trailhead sign. Knife's Edge was a vigorous 3.6-mile hike. Hikers were advised that the trail was steep in places with dangerous cliff faces and should use extreme caution. The trail was not recommended for beginner or intermediate hikers. All travelers were encouraged to use the logbook to sign in before starting up. Above the sign was a bright yellow handwritten sign that read, "Trail Closed".

Gracelyn ignored everything she'd read and started hiking.

13

MACK COOLEY
DIABLO POINT TRAIL

Present Day

"Are we on the same page?" Gracelyn asked again. Mack wanted to laugh in her face. What Gracelyn called "the same page" was really code for "Gracelyn's page".

"Sure," he said. "I get it. I'm backup and you're point person. We're going to enter through the exit of the tunnel, look for the snake. You're going to kill it—three shots to the head—and we'll retreat through the front of the tunnel if possible. If the way is unclear or unpassable, we'll retrace our steps and end up back here."

Gracelyn smiled slightly and took a big breath. "Yeah. That's it. Don't forget your ear protection."

She'd brought earplugs for them to put in when they got deeper into the tunnel. The gunshots underground would deafen them otherwise. Mack had taken the stringed earplugs when Gracelyn had handed them to him—she always kept extras of just about everything in her pack. He'd wondered if he would have the presence of mind to actually put them in.

That was the thing with Gracelyn: she only wanted to see how things could be. She thought if she lined everything up perfectly, that's how things would happen. As though by willing it to be a certain way, she could control the outcome. Mack was generally a fly-by-the-seat-of-your-pants type. But in this situation, all he could see were the ways things could go wrong. They were as obvious to him as warning notes on a map, in red ink.

The snake could be out of its lair. The bullets from Gracelyn's gun might not hit it. Or they might not be enough to kill it. She could very likely miss hitting it all together. Although she talked a good game, he knew that her eyesight in dim places like this was seriously compromised. They could get hurt in the tunnel and become dinner for the creature. They might—

"So, you ready?" Gracelyn asked. She'd pulled one of the two guns—the handgun—from her pack and held it loosely in her left hand. Mack was surprised how natural it looked there. She'd gotten it from Roger, she'd told him, and had been practicing with him. She could fire it, take it apart, clean it and put it back together with her eyes completely closed, Roger had told the family at dinner one night. He'd been obviously impressed. Gracelyn had just smiled and changed the subject.

"When you're in the tunnel you'll see what I mean," she'd told Mack earlier. "The light is really dim—even for a normal seeing person—and I don't want to be taken unaware."

"Why'd Roger agree to give you it?" Mack had asked. He knew Roger. He was a practical guy. Mack could hardly picture him offering to buy the used pistol for his sister, knowing what she intended to do with it.

"I told him I wanted it for self-defense on the trail," she'd said. "That'd I'd feel safer with it."

"And he didn't, I don't know, suggest a can of mace instead?" Mack had asked.

Gracelyn had just shaken her head, refusing to give him the satisfaction of a smile or laugh. She flexed her fingers on the gun's grip. Using the walking stick in her right hand, she swept the area in front of her slowly, carefully. It was a difficult task because they were trying to be quiet. The stick banged into rocks and bounced off boulders. Mack winced with every strike. Each noise was like a big, flashing neon sign to the snake, "here we are!".

Gracelyn stopped moving. "You go first," she motioned with the stick. "Please. Otherwise, I'm going to give us away. Here," she put the stick in his hand. "This could be an emergency weapon. But the second you see anything, any movement, let me get in front, okay?"

He was so surprised he only nodded dumbly.

Then, realizing she couldn't see him, whispered back, "All right."

They moved forward again. This time Gracelyn hung onto Mack's pack while he picked their course over the rocks and stones and around the occasional boulder. It was a narrow tunnel, enough that they had to walk hunched, with their packs on their backs like beetles. He'd love to flick on his flashlight or headlamp. The air was close and musty, smelling of old earth and worms. It was dry though and so far—

Mack's boot crunched loudly on something. He swore and glanced down. White stone lay broken under his foot. Whether it had already been smashed or his boot had done it he wasn't sure. He squinted as he looked down. Then pulled back instinctively.

"What is it?" Gracelyn's voice was barely audible.

"Bones," he said. "I just stepped on some bones. Probably just an old animal skeleton."

She was quiet a moment, then, "Let's keep going."

They walked on in silence again. How long was this tunnel? Mack wondered. Something sticky brushed over his face. A spiderweb clung to his eyelashes and coated his mouth and nose. He swept it away and then it stuck to his hand. Wiping it on his pant leg, Mack turned toward Gracelyn.

"Can I ask you something?" His whisper was so faint he wasn't sure she'd heard him.

"All right," she replied.

"Why now? It's been two years since...since everything happened. Why go after the snake now?"

She didn't say anything at first and he started walking again. But he felt her hand on his pack, tugging. He stopped again.

"They're going to re-open the trail," she whispered. "I found out from my brother who overhead it at the Town Office. There have been so many people up here exploring after...after what happened to my Dad that the authorities thought it was better to clear and re-open the trail. They're hoping to keep all the extra hikers safer." She snorted softly. "As if letting them up here with that thing is going to keep anyone safe."

Her voice was bitter and Mack couldn't blame her. She'd tried to get the town officials and the local authorities to believe her. They hadn't. They'd even had a town forum shortly after her father's body had been recovered. It was at the meeting, Gracelyn said, that a couple of others—mostly old-timers—had sworn that they too had seen or heard of the snake up on the mountain.

Those accounts had been silenced in patronizing tones by state officials and law enforcement, though. Experts had even been brought in for the meeting, Gracelyn had said, to prove that there was no possible or probable cause for a serpent to grow to such a large size. In the end, Emily had hauled her daughter out of the meeting, as Gracelyn had shouted that she wasn't lying, that there was something up there.

"She sounded like a lunatic," Gracelyn had overheard her mother tell Roger. "I just can't take much more of it."

After the funeral, Gracelyn had left. It was almost another year before she'd met him. And several months after that before Gracelyn had first opened up to Mack about it. He'd inadvertently found a news story about her. Just a short article from a national rag mag dredging up the Killer Snake around Halloween for some thrills and chills. He hadn't known what to do—she was so private he didn't want to scare her off. But he'd also felt like it would create a divide if he didn't say anything.

So, he'd asked her. And he'd learned in fits and starts the story of her and her father's trip up Diablo Point. And the fallout afterward.

"...better keep going," Gracelyn said.

Mack blinked. He started moving forward again, casting his eyes around the dim interior of the tunnel. He half-wished they'd make it all the way through the mountain without seeing a sign of the snake. And half-wished they'd see it now and get this over with. His stomach felt as though it were made of jelly and his mouth was pasty. He didn't dare try to get to his water bottle though.

He felt a jagged rock under his boot and adjusted his

footing. Two stones clinked together loudly. At first, he thought it had been him, that he'd knocked them with his foot. But then Mack realized that the sound had been a little further ahead and to their right. He swallowed and looked hard into the dimness ahead of them. He could see the faint outline of stones and boulders, and periodically the exposed strands of roots overhead. A smell reached his nose now, one that he'd noticed faintly before. Like dead things.

"I hear something," Gracelyn whispered.

The tunnel was silent for three breaths. Then four. Then there was another clunk, again from the right.

"It's there," Gracelyn said. "Can you see it?"

Mack squinted. He couldn't see anything. But that didn't mean there wasn't anything there. He swept his stick out in front of him, wishing it were a torch.

"I don't—" Mack's words died away. There, to the right side of the tunnel's walls, two glowing eyes stared back at them.

14

GRACELYN EDWARDS

KNIFE'S EDGE TRAIL

Two Years Ago

S he'd been hiking more than an hour and Gracelyn wished she'd taken time to go home before she'd started and swapped out her sneakers for boots. Or at least grabbed a bottle of water at a gas station. Her throat was dry and dusty feeling, her toes ached where they'd banged into rocks and stones. Even though Knife's Edge was a maintained trail, that didn't mean there weren't obstacles. Occasional deadfall had to be gotten over or around. And rocks and stones poked up through the ground on most of the path.

Gracelyn used her impromptu walking stick in front of her, whacking it against downed limbs and larger rocks before her shins hit them. She focused on the potential obstacles in front of her, but her mind kept straying back to the tunnel.

She could still see it so clearly: her father's look of horror when the snake had first emerged from the darkness. She could hear his yell for her to get out, to run. Goosebumps ran down her sweaty arms and she pushed the thoughts away. She'd be no good to him if she melted into a blubbering, bawling puddle. She had to keep her head. Maintain her focus.

A branch snapped nearby and Gracelyn stopped, swiveled in that direction. The leaves and trees around her were blurred but she could make out the shapes enough to see if someone—or something—was moving.

Swallowing, Gracelyn listened. Again, there was the rustle of leaves and the sound of small branches underfoot. Something was moving in the woods just beyond her line of sight. She sniffed the air. She couldn't smell anything but it could be she was standing upwind from whatever it was.

Should she call out, warn it away? But if it was one of the searchers—

"Hey! What are you doing out here?" a voice, male and older—maybe her father's age—sounded from a ways off. Gracelyn considered running for it but discarded the idea. Whoever it was would likely be faster in the forest than she was, especially on an unfamiliar trail.

"Who are you?" Gracelyn asked, her voice more hostile than she'd intended.

More snaps and the sound of feet moving through dead leaves. "Bob Haley. I'm in charge of the volunteers with the local search and rescue group. This trail's closed."

"Oh."

The man drew closer. Now, Gracelyn could smell his scent: a mix of sweat and some kind of piney bug repellant.

"We've got a...a missing hiker," Bob said. "The trails around here are all closed. I'm surprised you didn't see the signs."

"I must have overlooked them," Gracelyn said.

He was drawing closer but she still couldn't make him out.

"You hiking?" he asked. She wondered what else he thought she'd be doing out in the woods.

"Yeah. Just a quick one. Meeting some friends later."

"Not today, miss. No hikers on the trails in this part of the forest. It could compromise any artifacts left by the missing man."

Gracelyn's heart thumped so loudly she was surprised Bob couldn't hear it.

"I—" but she was interrupted by the sound of a short-wave radio.

The voice was muffled but she caught, "...repeat...hiker..."

Gracelyn's stomach dropped.

"Haley to Eagle, repeat that please," Bob said into the radio. He fumbled with the radio, made an adjustment.

"The, uh, hiker you're looking for. Is that Shawn Edwards?" Gracelyn asked.

Bob didn't respond.

It was silent a moment before the radio squawked again with some static and more garbled speech. Bob silenced it. Gracelyn could feel him studying her.

"Wait a minute. Are you his kid? The daughter that was hiking with him?" He swore softly under his breath. "You'd better come with me."

"Eagle to Haley. Repeat. All units back to base. Missing hiker has been located. All units are to return to base."

Gracelyn felt a warm, happy glow spread in her chest. She felt lighter too, as though a physical weight had been lifted from her shoulders. Dad was all right. They'd found him.

Bob waited for the voice to stop and then said, "Haley to

Eagle, 10-4. I have the daughter here. Bringing her in with me."

"Roger that, Haley."

Gracelyn followed Bob but wanted to shove past him, run ahead. She wanted to find the voice on the other end of that radio and demand it put her father on the radio. Was he conscious? She wanted him to see her face when he woke up. Why was Bob walking so slowly?

"Can we pick up the pace a little?" Gracelyn asked Bob's back. He didn't reply but moved a little faster. She could hear him breathing, regular and even with an occasional whistle of air in his throat. She wondered if he'd been a smoker. Or was an asthmatic.

The terrain off-trail was rough and uneven. Bob didn't talk other than to point out more deadfall or other significant obstacles in Gracelyn's way. She appreciated the fact that he didn't coddle her. If he knew who she was then he must also know that she was blind.

A branch ahead of Bob swung back and narrowly missed her face.

"Sorry about that," he said. "Few more minutes and we'll be back to base."

"Is that where he is? My dad? Or have they already taken him to the hospital?"

"Not sure," Bob grunted as he moved over something large. "Watch this log."

Gracelyn clambered over the thick trunk of a downed tree.

"Can you ask?" she said.

"We're almost back. Then you'll get all the information you need."

Gracelyn pressed her lips together. Almost there. She could practically see her father's face. He'd be tired of course, maybe some broken bones. But he'd be there and she could tell him how sorry she was. That she'd left. That she'd ever come up with the idea of visiting Diablo Point, to begin with.

Fifteen minutes later they connected to a trail and five minutes after that it spit them onto one of the dirt roads that ran through the Vermont National Forest. The big motor she'd heard earlier was getting louder and louder. As soon as her feet hit the dirt road she started to run awkwardly on her sprained ankle toward the sound.

"Hey!" Bob called but she ignored him and kept running.

The sun was high overhead and a line of sweat ran down Gracelyn's forehead and over her nose. She ignored it and pumped her legs faster. Her ankle throbbed and screamed at her to stop but she ignored it, too.

"Dad?" she yelled. "Dad, I'm coming!"

When she reached the pull off on the road where the mobile Search and Rescue unit had been set up, there were a lot of people around. They were quiet though, probably tired after their ordeal. She stopped the first person she saw, an older woman with short gray hair and an ugly pea soup colored T-shirt.

"Please, I'm looking for my father. Shawn. Shawn Edwards. Do you know where he is?"

"I—" the woman sounded startled, her eyes were wide.

Gracelyn wanted to shake her.

"I think you'd better talk to Sheriff Johnson."

"I don't want to talk with anyone but my father," Gracelyn said, her voice high and breathless. She could sense movement around her, people drew closer. Gawkers, like she was an accident in the road or a downed animal that had met its fate with some truck's tires.

"Look, if you can just—"

"Gracelyn Edwards?" a man's voice asked from behind her. It was a deep voice and commanded authority.

"Yes." She turned. The man in front of her wore a sheriff's star over his breast pocket. Above it was a blurry line of script that she assumed read Sheriff someone or other.

"We have some questions you'll need to answer. Please, come this way," he held out a hand toward her.

Gracelyn swatted it away. "I need to see my father. Where is he?"

"Please, Ms. Edwards. If you'll just come with me. We have some questions—"

"I don't care about your stupid questions!" Gracelyn's voice was high and loud. She shouldn't panic. Couldn't panic, not now. She took a breath, tried to calm down. "Please, sheriff. I need to speak to my dad. If you'd just give me a few minutes with him, I—"

"I'm sorry, but that won't be possible." The sheriff paused, cleared his throat. "I'm very sorry, Ms. Edwards, but your father didn't make it out alive. We recovered his body in the woods. Rescue is bringing him down now. I've been in contact with your mother and—"

"No. No, that's not right. That isn't possible. I was just with him—just hours ago. He can't be dead. They must have it wrong. He could be unconscious. Did they even check? Did they—"

Gracelyn covered her face with her hands. She was surprised to find her cheeks were wet. Her shoulder shook and a big, warm hand covered one of them, guiding her away from the people and the tent.

～

"WE'VE BEEN over this twenty times! What don't you get?" Gracelyn's voice was thin, high and strained. She'd been sitting across from Sheriff Johnson and Officer Jakes for the past two hours. They'd questioned her first up on the mountain, then had taken her back to the same smelly, cramped office where she'd sat hours before. Gracelyn rubbed a hand over her face. It felt gritty with leftover dirt and dried tears.

She refused to think about anything other than the questions she was being asked. Refused to think about her father or the body that they claimed to have found in the woods. In the woods? That didn't even make sense. The snake had grabbed him in the tunnel. So, why would her father's body be out in the woods? They were lying. Gracelyn just wasn't sure why.

"We just want to make sure that we have all the facts straight. You said that when you last saw your father, you were in a tunnel toward the top of Diablo Point?"

"Yes."

"And he had been, uh, attacked by a large reptile."

"A snake. Yes. It...it paralyzed him with its venom. At least, I think that's what happened. It snagged him with its tail and..." she let her voice drift off as she heard the sheriff shuffling papers on the desk. Tweedledum and Tweedledee hadn't made a great impression so far. She knew they were just doing their jobs but honestly if this was the quality of law enforcement in the area, it was a wonder any of the citizens lived into their seventies.

There was a knock at the door. Sheriff Johnson was sitting closest and got up to answer it. Someone stood outside but the door blocked them.

A woman's voice, low asked, "Her mother is asking when you might be finished. Wants to know when the girl will be released."

"Shouldn't be much longer. Offer her some coffee."

"I did but I'll ask again."

The door closed.

Gracelyn stood up. "I'm done here."

"We just have a few more questions—"

"No. If I'm not under arrest then I'm leaving. Am I?"

Sheriff Johnson was silent but put his hands on his hips. Officer Jakes sat absolutely still.

"Are you what?" the sheriff asked.

"Am I under arrest?"

There was a momentary pause. "No. But you are a person of interest."

Gracelyn swayed slightly on her feet. She reached for the desk in front of her.

"And why is that?"

"Because, Ms. Edwards, you were the last person to see your father alive."

"And that makes me guilty of his death?"

The words felt so strange on her tongue. Her father was dead. Dad. Dead. She shook her head.

"It puts you under suspicion, yes. We certainly aren't ready to charge you with anything. Yet."

"Well, until you do I believe I'm free to go. Isn't that true?"

Officer Jakes started to speak but the sheriff motioned with his hand.

"Yes, that's true." His voice was quiet. Resigned.

"Thank you so much," Gracelyn said, her voice a mix of shakiness and sarcasm. "I'll see myself out."

But Sheriff Johnson opened the door for her. Gracelyn passed through it without looking at him. She found the same chair rail and followed the arrowed signs that read, "reception" in the opposite direction as the door where she and Mom had left the building last time. The hallway eventually ended in an austere waiting room filled with hard blue chairs.

Her mother stood alone by a smeared window, looking out at the parking lot.

"Mom?" Gracelyn said, her voice wobbling. All the anger left her suddenly and she felt like a deflated balloon.

Her mother turned. Her face was blotchy and red, her eyes swollen. Gracelyn expected her mother to run to her, wrap her in her arms. She wanted that suddenly, achingly hard. For her mother to hug her and tell her that everything was going to be all right. That there had been a mistake and Dad was waiting for them in the car or at the hospital.

Instead, her mother stood and stared at her as though she couldn't really see Gracelyn. When Mom spoke her voice was barely more than a whisper.

"Let's go," was all she said before she turned and walked toward the door.

15

MACK COOLEY

DIABLO POINT

Present Day

"Can you—" Gracelyn repeated but Mack put his hand behind him and gripped her forearm. She went silent. The eyes, still glowing were immobile.

He turned his body slightly toward Gracelyn and whispered in her ear. "To our right, ahead about three yards. Maybe more."

She nodded. He could feel her head bobbing under his lips. Her body was silent but her breathing had increased. Mack's own heart was banging hard into his ribs.

"Ready?" he whispered.

Gracelyn nodded. Mack readied the high-powered flashlight. When the snake was close enough for a clean shot, he'd raise it and aim the beam directly at the snake's head. Gracelyn would use that as her signal and take the shots she needed.

"Put on your ear protection," she whispered, her breath warm on his cheek. He pulled the earplugs from the cord around his neck and put them into his ears. The cave had been quiet other than the slight noise of rocks clinking together as they'd walked. Now it was so silent his ears started to ring.

He watched the wall intently. The eyes hadn't moved. Mack held his breath.

Why wasn't it moving? Couldn't it see or smell them? They were close enough to take a shot but Gracelyn's chances of hitting it only grew better the closer they were. Still, how close could they get before spooking it?

"Go," Gracelyn whispered and pressed gently on Mack's shoulder. He moved forward, keeping his eyes flicking between the rocky ground underfoot and the right side of the tunnel.

No movement.

He took a few more steps.

Nothing except the dark eyes staring.

Two more steps.

Then a strange sound filled the air. Half moan, half cry. It came from the snake. The eyes trembled slightly. It was studying them, Mack realized with horror.

"Now!" he yelled and lifted up the flashlight, shining the bright light in the snake's eyes. Gracelyn raised the gun and was about to fire.

But something was wrong.

"No, Gracelyn, don't!"

She stopped. He heard her swear under her breath, saw her flinch and lower her hand.

"It's not the snake. It's..." His voice drifted off as he moved closer to the animal, unsure what he was seeing.

It was a raccoon Mack realized, but it was all wrong. Its

body was twisted and contorted. As though it had been knotted up and pinned to the side of the tunnel. Mack remembered the butterfly mounts that he'd made in seventh grade. The way that the fragile wings had fluttered against the velvety board until they'd stopped moving. The raccoon made another weak moaning, chirping sound as they drew closer.

"What's happened to it?" Mack asked. Even the whisper sounded too loud in the tight space.

"The snake got it. It has that paralyzing venom or whatever it is, that comes out of its tail. It must stick the animal with it, come back later to eat it."

Mack frowned. He'd heard of this behavior before—mostly in insects, mostly arachnids—but a reptile? Still. Who'd ever heard of a gigantic snake-like Gracelyn had seen?

The small, furry animal was alive but was stunned or in a trance.

"It's suffering," Gracelyn said. She pointed to a thick band of blood that covered part of the raccoon's body. There was a gash there, fresh blood oozed out of it.

Mack pulled the knife from his belt and in one clean, quick motion, plunged it into the raccoon's neck. It was stiff, as though rigor mortis had already set in. Gracelyn said something quietly under her breath that Mack didn't hear.

Another sound filled the tunnel. Something ahead of them. Coming their way. A slow, low sliding sound.

"It's coming," she said.

They waited, not moving, not even daring to blink. Mack felt the knife tremble in his hand. He held it in front of him. Just in case, he thought. Just in case she misses.

But the sound was all wrong. It was getting quieter, not louder.

"It's going the other way," Gracelyn said, her voice a loud whisper. "Go. Quick!"

Mack flicked the light back off. They were plunged into instant darkness and squiggles danced in front of his eyes while they adjusted. The walls of the tunnel seemed to constrict, the air grew hotter.

He scrambled quickly and quietly over the stones and rocks and who knew what else that littered the cave floor. It took more than a minute for his eyes to adjust to the darkness again. And Gracelyn must be having an even harder time. He wanted to ask her if he should put the light back on but worried they were already making too much noise. Had they scared the snake away?

Mack stopped suddenly and listened.

"I don't hear it," Gracelyn said. "Do you?"

The tunnel was silent as a crypt.

"No."

She swore and kicked a rock nearby. "We can't let it get away. Who knows when it will come back. It might have another lair somewhere else. It could be days before it returns, maybe weeks."

They started forward again in an uncomfortable half crawl, half jog. "Just turn the stupid light on," Gracelyn said. "It already knows we're here."

Mack flicked on the bright beam once again. It illuminated the tunnel ahead of them which was indeed growing narrower. How long was this thing anyway? More cobwebs brushed his cheeks but he ignored them. They ran until the tunnel narrowed so much that they had to stop.

"Do you think we could get through without the packs?" Mack asked. He was bent over double, peering through the ever-narrowing tunnel ahead of them. The air here was dank and smelled of mustiness and something rotting.

"If we back out and go around to the front there's no way we'll catch up with it."

Mack nodded but his stomach twisted painfully. The thought of leaving his pack and crawling on his hands and knees through the tunnel made his lungs tighten. The earthen walls, already heavy around them, would feel more so when they were touching their bare skin, pressing down overhead.

"It's your call," he said.

Gracelyn answered without hesitation. "Yes, go."

Mack squatted, pulled his pack off gently and laid it on the path. Gracelyn did the same.

"You know this means we won't have any backup measures," he said.

"I know," she said, her voice soft. "So I'll just have to make sure I don't miss."

A single trickle of sweat slid down Mack's back and into his waistband.

"All right," he said. "Let's go."

"Mack, wait," Gracelyn said. He stopped, turned around. She unclipped the short-barreled shotgun from her pack and handed it to him. Her fingers brushed his and he felt them tremble before she removed them. "Take this. In case I miss."

"You won't," Mack said, but took the gun and strapped it crosswise over his back. He started to crawl through the dank tunnel.

WHY WOULD IT FLEE? The thought spun around and around in Gracelyn's mind like a record on a turntable. It made no sense. There were two of them, miniatures in comparison to the snake. So why would it turn and run?

Unless it wasn't running. It could be leading them into a trap.

Gracelyn paused mid-crawl. Her skin was coated with dirt and cobwebs, her breath coming fast in her chest.

Was that it? Was the snake not running away from them, but leading them somewhere else? Dammit! Maybe they should have gone around by the outside of the mountain to the front of the tunnel, tried their luck that way. But if the snake was really leaving—going to another lair—it would be long gone before they ever made it back around to the front entrance.

It was becoming hard to breathe. The air was so stale and flat it seemed to be oxygen-depleted. Gracelyn imagined telling Mack to forget this, to turn back. They were crawling on hands and knees. The tunnel had become even more narrow—she hadn't thought that was possible—and there was a good chance they'd get stuck. Then what? They'd be easy pickings for the snake or anything else that visited this hole underground.

Gracelyn shook her head.

No.

They weren't going to turn tail and run. And they weren't helpless here. They had weapons. And brains. They'd be fine.

Are you sure? a little voice in her mind asked. *Look what happened to your father.*

Gracelyn felt red anger glow hot in her chest.

"Can you go any faster?" she whispered to Mack.

"Not really," he said over his shoulder. "I...see....har...going." Half his words were lost in the thick, dead air.

Gracelyn watched the light bounce around in the tunnel

ahead of Mack. The beam was so powerful it bleached everything in its path. She wanted to climb over Mack, take the lead. She wasn't used to following and hated admitting that she needed help from anyone, even Mack. Especially Mack.

"...a bend...ahead...pretty sharp."

"OK." She stayed close on his heels. Her knees ached from scrabbling over the rough, stony ground. Her hands, she was sure, were cut and bruised. She grunted and pushed on.

She wouldn't go back defeated.

If you go back at all, the little voice whispered again. Gracelyn hated that voice. It had taken up residence after her father...after the accident.

"...ready...turn. Not sure...how...fit..." Mack's voice interrupted. It was hard to make out, the words drifting in and out of her ears.

He stopped abruptly and Gracelyn barely missed face planting in his backside. His hiking boot hit her in the sternum.

"Sorry," he said. "I'm stuck."

"What?"

"The shotgun...caught...something..."

Gracelyn felt around in front of her. Her hand connected with Mack's well-muscled calves, his quads, his buttocks and finally his back. He was struggling to free the gun, one of his hands grabbed the air around it, tried to adjust the strap.

"Here," she whispered and climbed practically onto his back. The ceiling of the tunnel pushed down on her, like giant, dirty hands. She felt around the strap and found where it was twisted. It had made the rifle jut out at an angle, catching on the side of the tunnel wall. She could feel the twist in the thick leather strap but couldn't smooth it out from her awkward angle.

Mack shifted under her. She could feel his body vibrating slightly. He must be as tired as she was.

"Hold still," she said, her voice a thin whisper. She could barely breathe. The ceiling of the cave was pressing the air out of her lungs.

"Gracelyn," Mack whispered hoarsely. "It's—"

Gracelyn heard it moving. Close, so close she could almost taste it. The sound of a large, slippery body moving over the rough terrain.

Moving toward them.

Fast.

16

GRACELYN EDWARDS

GLACIER NATIONAL PARK

Four Months after Shawn's Death

"Why did I let you talk me into this?" Nina groaned her head in her hands. Gracelyn smiled at Jen who sat behind the steering wheel of her 1978 Volkswagen bus.

"It's going to be great," Jen said, glancing back at Nina in the rearview mirror. "The experience of a lifetime."

"Yeah, right. The last experience of my lifetime."

Jen laughed, snorting as she did so.

"Chill, Nina." She put the blinker on, slowed for a stop sign. Another sign nearby directed tourists to Wild Glaciers River Runners. "Did you or did you not just climb Granite Peak?" She waited for a response but Nina was silent from the back seat.

"Yes, Jen, I did," Jen said in a higher-than-normal voice. "Because I'm fierce."

Gracelyn smiled more deeply at that. "Fierce" had

become the trio's buzz word. It was used when they were huddled in their tents on steeply pitched mountainsides in pouring rainstorms and when they'd come across a bear— an uninterested one, thankfully—at the base of the mountains they'd climbed a few weeks ago. The word had been used to dare each other to test their limits—each one of them in turn—and had been tossed around the campfire when they massaged their blistered feet and shared stories of bravado. "Fierce" hadn't described Gracelyn just a year ago. Then, she'd been outwardly brave—scaling peaks in the northeast, alone sometimes, sometimes with other solo hikers. Inwardly, she'd been a mess. Thoughts of her father and his death and her role in it plagued her.

She'd given up her blog about mysterious creatures watching with disinterest as the ad revenue and other affiliate income had started to nosedive. She'd worked odd jobs instead, saving money for food and gear for the trails. The trails. That was her focus and had been since she'd left Bondville. She tried not to think about her mother and brother, what their faces must have looked like when they'd found her letter the day after her father's funeral. She'd packed lightly, snuck out of the house before dawn and walked until a commuter had picked her up. From there, Gracelyn had crisscrossed the state, then other parts of New England. She wasn't sure what she was searching for other than relief. And when she was gasping for breath as she pounded up a mountain or holding it as she searched for footfalls on steep descents, it was easier to block out everything else.

"It could be worse," she'd told her mother on one of her infrequent phone calls home. "I could have become an addict."

Mom had sighed. Gracelyn had pictured her rubbing a

hand wearily over her eyes. "You are an addict, Gracelyn," she'd said. "It's just that your drug of choice is adrenaline. Please, come home." Mom always ended their calls with those three words. Or maybe that had simply become a sign for Gracelyn that it was time to hang up.

"I'll be home soon," she always replied. But never meant it.

"This is going to be a blast," Jen said now. Gracelyn glanced out the window and caught her breath.

Again.

Montana was the most beautiful place she'd ever seen. The mountains made those in New England look like tiny hills, the rugged beauty of the landscape here was jaw-dropping. And that was all seen through her smeared vision. She couldn't imagine what it must look like for her friends.

She craned her neck back, smiled at Nina. Her face was blurry in the back seat where it was darker but Gracelyn could tell Nina looked nervous. She was usually confident on the trail and didn't mind sharing her opinion. In fact, it had been Nina who'd been unsure Gracelyn would be a good fit. "Nothing personal, but you know the old saying, 'three's a crowd'."

Jen and Nina had been hiking in Maine, finishing up the last section of the Appalachian Trail, while Gracelyn had been hiking Mount Katanin, the highest mountain in the state. The three women had met along the way to the top. Mount Katanin was the northernmost part of the AT.

It had been Jen's idea, after several hours of hiking together and a shared lunch on the summit, to invite Gracelyn along on the women's next adventure. She was the more impulsive of the two.

"I'd love to," Gracelyn had responded when Jen had blurted it out over a bag of Cheetos bought specifically to celebrate the duos completion of the last mountain on the trail. "But you barely know me."

"I can tell you're good people," Jen had said with a smile. "Plus, we need one more to share the driving." They'd been talking for the last hour about their plans next: a trip out west to Montana to spend time hiking smaller mountains and finally, Granite Peak.

Gracelyn had felt her stomach drop. She'd had an easy time hiding her vision loss on the trail. The day was fiercely sunny and bright and though the forest looked slightly blurred, it had been easy to pick out obstacles and move around them without the aid of a walking stick. She'd swallowed. Maybe she could fake it...the thought had barely formed before Gracelyn tossed it aside.

As a teen, unable to deal with the fact she was losing her vision, Gracelyn had taken her parents' car one gloomy Sunday afternoon. A wreck had resulted in a broken arm and a totaled Toyota. It had also confirmed that she couldn't get behind the wheel anymore.

Gracelyn shook her head and pulled herself from the old memories. Here they were, many weeks after Maine and so many trails together, she'd lost track of them all. Nina and Jen were her family now. They didn't know much about her—she rarely shared about her past—but they knew her now. And really, wasn't that more important than anyone's history?

"Let's leave everything here until we figure out what we're doing," Jen said. Gracelyn heard another moan from Nina in the back but she opened the door and climbed out. Gracelyn followed.

The air smelled of green things growing and slightly fishy from the churning water nearby. The river was blue and sparkled in the early morning sun.

"I can't believe we're doing this," Nina mumbled as she and Gracelyn followed Jen who was yards ahead toward the visitor center. "Worst idea ever."

"You'll be fine," Gracelyn said. "Plus, you get next choice."

They'd been taking turns for the past few months, choosing destinations by turn. After Granite Peak, Gracelyn had chosen a four-day fast hike through some of Montana's most rugged wilderness. It had rained three out of the four days and they'd used their fierce mantra frequently to keep them going. Next, it was Nina's turn to pick something. Gracelyn had a feeling it wouldn't be water-related.

"Jen hates me. This is why she's doing this. She knows that water and I don't get along."

"Weren't you on the swim team at your school or something?"

Nina laughed, a quick hard bark of humor. "No, that was Jen."

"Oh."

"I do know how to swim. I took lessons in my neighbor's pool for like six years."

"Ah."

"I just hate the thought of falling out of the raft. I mean, what if I hit my head and am unconscious or something?"

"I think we're going to get helmets."

"Still." Nina stopped walking suddenly. "Hang on."

Gracelyn waited, assuming Nina had forgotten something in the van.

"I may have just had a change of heart," Nina said. "Talk about trail candy."

"We're not on a trail," Gracelyn smiled.

"Well, I think he just emerged from one. And he's looking very delectable."

Gracelyn looked in the same direction as Nina. She saw Jen, stopped ahead and chatting with a guy about their age. He was blurry from this distance, but Gracelyn could make out a fit, muscular frame. Tanned bare arms poking out of his T-shirt. Sandy brown curls and a wide, white smile.

"Holy hail Mary," Nina breathed. "I'm ready to get in the raft."

The man nodded at something Jen was saying, then motioned with his arm toward the river. Jen said a few more things and he nodded again. Then he turned back toward another small group of people and Jen started back toward Gracelyn and Nina.

"You did really well out there today," Mack said, sitting down on one of the stumps around the campfire. The light danced and swayed, beautiful but challenging for Gracelyn to make out features or faces.

She smiled, not looking away from the flames. "Thanks," she said.

"You must have done this before." He paused, sipped from a can of microbrew in his hand. Gracelyn stirred, took a sip from her own can. It had grown warm in her hand.

"No, it was my first time. But I liked it."

Mack chuckled. "I could tell."

"Have you been doing this long?"

"Not in Montana. I haven't been here that long. But I led a lot of groups in Colorado, some in northern California. Same general skills, just different water."

Gracelyn nodded. "Ever go rafting in New England?" She didn't know why she felt her cheeks stained pink. She wasn't inviting him. Just curious.

He paused. Took a sip of his beer. "No, I haven't. Yet. That where you're from?"

Gracelyn nodded and rubbed her hands over her arms. The night air was brisk, even after the heat of the midday sun.

"Here, take this," Mack said and handed her the fleece jacket that had been laying across his knees.

"Oh, no. That's—"

"Just take it," he grinned. She could see the white flash in the firelight though his other facial features were too blurred to make out. She hesitated, then took the jacket and slipped it over her shoulders. It felt good, warm and soft and smelled faintly of some woodsy scent.

"Thanks."

"Sure," Mack said. "How long are you in town for?"

"Not long. We'd planned to just stay a couple more days after this river trip. Do some of the lower elevations."

"And then it's back to New England? Vermont, right? I remember now."

"No. I mean, yes, that's where I'm originally from but no, we aren't heading back that way anytime soon. Jen has a lead on a job at a state park—their outdoor education center teacher just bailed—so we'll be going out to Wyoming next."

Mack didn't say anything at first. Then, "It's beautiful out there. Funny thing, that's where I'm headed in a few weeks."

Gracelyn's heart skipped a beat then resumed its natural rhythm.

"Really?" She hoped her voice didn't give her away.

"Yeah. This is the busy season and the guy that owns the place told me he wouldn't need me for the entire season. They stay open until fall, but it starts to slow down in a couple of weeks. It's good timing."

She could feel his eyes move from the fire to her. She ignored it and continued staring into the flames.

"What part," he asked, "of Wyoming?"

"Up around Jackson. I forget the name."

"Oh yeah? Huh. That's where I'm headed. Jackson."

Gracelyn couldn't help but smile. Her stomach flip-flopped in a way that it hadn't for a really long time. *Don't be stupid. Now isn't a good time to get involved.*

"What a coincidence," she said.

Mack was still smiling at her but now leaned back in his chair, draping one arm over the back of it. "Sure is. Maybe we could meet up when I get there, do some hiking together."

Gracelyn paused. "I don't know."

He half snorted, half laughed. "You're a tough cookie."

Gracelyn laughed too and the sound startled her. Among their little threesome, she'd earned the title of Glum Gracelyn. Getting her to laugh was a challenge that Jen took on—and failed—almost every day.

"I've heard that once before," she said and poked at the burning logs with a nearby stick.

"I like it," Mack said. His chair creaked as he got to his feet. "I'm getting another beer. Can I get you anything?"

"No, thanks."

He moved off into the darkness of the camp. Gracelyn's heart pounded harder than necessary for someone sitting down and relaxing.

Don't do this. Don't be stupid. This isn't the right time to get involved.

But Gracelyn only smiled and poked the fire once more, making the sparks fly up into the dark sky.

17

GRACELYN EDWARDS

THE TUNNEL, DIABLO POINT

Present Day

The sound of something large and slippery moving over the rough terrain filled the tunnel.

It was getting closer. Everything in Gracelyn said *run, run, run. Get out of there.* Instead, she yanked harder on the rifle's strap. It let go suddenly and Mack collapsed under her momentarily. She pushed forward and crawled her way in front of him. Or tried to.

"Don't!" he shouted. He shoved her back, blocked her way.

It was hard to put together what happened next. Like the fragments of the event were scattered before her; a jigsaw puzzle jumbled in a mass of pieces.

She had the pistol in her left hand. She needed light. *Light, Mack, where was the light?* She couldn't see anything. Couldn't see around him. His body filled the narrow space of the tunnel. But she could hear the quick slithering: the body of the snake moving closer. It sounded like someone with rough hands caressing a piece of silk fabric.

Then, an explosion. A burst of hot orange light from the short-barreled shotgun loaded with mini shells. She saw Mack's body for a single second. He jerked only slightly from the recoil. Still, one of his boots hit her in the shoulder. She cried out but couldn't hear it. It felt like sirens filled her ears when the shotgun discharged in the enclosed space. Then a ringing filled her head.

She scrambled forward. Tried again to get in front of Mack. Suddenly, he wasn't there anymore. Gracelyn's shoulders heaved. Was she crying? Breathing? Screaming? She was helpless. The realization dawned quickly. She couldn't see or hear anything in the narrow space under the earth. She put her hands out in front of her. Knocked the one with the pistol against the tunnel's walls. The other hand clawed out in front, searching for Mack. But her hand came away empty again and again.

Where was he?

A choking mushroom cloud of panic fell over her. He was going to die. Just like her father. Because of her.

Stop it. Stop it! Get yourself together, idiot!

She kept pushing forward, kept feeling out with her hands. Any second she expected to feel cool scales under her fingers. Or for her palms to bump against the thick coil of the snake's body. But the tunnel was empty. She pressed on, banging out a kind of rhythm with her feet and hands as she crawled forward. Something feathery touched her cheek—a spider? A web? A root?—she didn't wait to find out.

Her right hand hit something smooth and metallic feeling. The flashlight. She could have kissed it. She flicked the light on. The light was warm and yellow and so welcome she almost cried. She flicked it around, from right to left, behind her then back ahead again.

The tunnel was empty.

She had the flashlight.

So, where was Mack?

Gracelyn stuck the pistol into the back of her waistband so she could crawl faster.

Thump, thump, thump. The flashlight bumped over the bare ground underneath her hands and knees. She could feel the reverberations but still couldn't hear anything. Her head felt stuffed full of wool.

The tunnel took a sharp turn. Gracelyn wedged herself into the space and felt something with lots of legs skitter over an exposed swath of skin on her back.

Breathe. One, two, three, four, five... Panicking would cause her to make dumb mistakes. She continued counting every time her hand touched the ground in front of her.

...nine, ten, eleven.

She forced herself to breathe more slowly even though it felt hard to breathe at all. She'd made it through the snug turn in the tunnel. Now it was straighter again and widening.

...fourteen, fifteen, sixteen.

Gracelyn felt something brush against her arm. A root poking through the ground above swayed as she moved past it.

...twenty-one, twenty-two, twenty—

What was that? A sound—from far away, or maybe close by, Gracelyn's ears weren't registering—filled the tunnel.

Was it a yell?

Mack!

Gracelyn plowed on faster, wedging the flashlight between her chin and chest so that both hands were free.

She scrabbled over the earth, the smell of worms and minerals and decomposing things thick in her nose. The smell was getting stronger. The scent of death, the same as the rear of the tunnel.

She paused for a second, listened hard.

Nothing.

Mack. Mack, I'm coming!

She scuttled on, sweat making her shirt stick to her chest and back. It dripped in her eyes but she didn't bother taking time to wipe it away.

Mack. Mack, I'm coming...

The words had become a mantra, repeated over and over in her mind like fingers over a rosary.

Mack. Mack, I'm—

Then, ahead. The tunnel changed.

Gracelyn stopped abruptly.

It couldn't be.

The tunnel had ended.

Here it was wide enough for her to stand as long as she remained bent over. Light—sunlight—poured in from the large hole in front of her further ahead. Gracelyn stood, her mouth slightly open and stared.

It was the entrance of the tunnel on the far side of the cave. Where she and Dad had been that day. She blinked, tried to clear the images of him as he looked then from her mind. She could see him all around her: standing by the entrance of the cave; reaching for her, trying to pull her back; then his body twisting as he shouted for her to run...

Gracelyn panted. She put her hands over her aching ears and moaned.

If the tunnel was empty, then where was the snake?

And where was Mack?

GRACELYN WAS fifteen years old when she'd noticed a change in her vision. She's always worn glasses —the only one in her family who needed them—and at first, Mom thought she just needed a stronger prescription. Gracelyn had transitioned into contact lenses by then, begging her father. He'd caved a week after her thirteenth birthday. Contact lenses weren't covered by insurance the same way glasses were, but he'd worked some overtime and gotten her the contacts.

Her optometrist, a geriatric man—at least to a fifteen-year-old—with a wobbly gray mustache, had warned her that some people's eyes just didn't like contact lenses. "There are cases," he'd said, "where glasses are the way to go."

That day, he'd started with the regular eye test: "Which line of letters can you see?" and moved onto some others: blowing air into her eyeballs to test for glaucoma and a series involving bright lights and reading letters and numbers until her eyes were tired and slightly sore.

Then he'd brought Mom into the room.

Uh-oh, Gracelyn had thought. *This can't be good.* She dreaded the news. She must be one of those special few whose eyes didn't like contacts. She'd clenched her fists, the frustration already building. She hated glasses. Hated the way they slid down her nose greasily when she got too warm while playing sports or running outdoors. Hated their heaviness and the way they pinched her nose.

The doctor had cleared his throat. "Mrs. Edwards. Gracelyn. I'm afraid I have some rather...unexpected results from today's tests."

The room had been silent other than the overly-loud tick of an ugly cat clock on the far wall.

"Yes?" Gracelyn's mother had finally said.

"I...well. There's no easy way to say this I'm afraid."

Just say it. Glasses forever. Her palms burned and she realized she'd been digging her nails into them.

"Now, these are just preliminary tests, you understand. We'll need to do a full workup to be certain these findings are accurate—"

"What is it?" Gracelyn had finally blurted out. "I'm going to be stuck with glasses again, right?"

"No, it's not that," the doctor had said. His mustache wagged with the words. She thought not for the first time how much it resembled a fuzzy caterpillar.

"I'm afraid it's more serious," he'd continued. "The tests indicate that something more significant is going on. There is severe deterioration..."

After that, the words all blurred together. Gracelyn heard things like, "continued worsening," and "months, maybe at best," and then, "juvenile macular degeneration," and then finally, "blindness."

Blindness?

The word swirled around her like a tornado, blocking everything else out. She'd tried to refocus, to hear the questions that her mother was asking. Mom's voice had shaken like leaves in the wind and Gracelyn recognized the thick sound of tears in her words.

But the single word beat like a drumbeat in Gracelyn's skull, deafening her.

Blindness. Blindness. Blindness.

When they'd left the office, Gracelyn had been supporting her mother's arm. It had been Gracelyn—with a stronger prescription contact lenses—that had dug in her mother's purse for the insurance card. Gracelyn who'd shaken her head dumbly when the receptionist asked, "Do you usually have a copay?" And who'd told the receptionist to call her mother later to schedule the next round of tests.

Gracelyn had driven them home. She'd gotten her learner's permit on her fifteenth birthday, barely passing after she'd hit the curb during the parallel parking. She'd bounded into the house and into her father's arms with a huge smile on her face that day.

Blindness.

When they were halfway home, Gracelyn started shaking, every bit of her trembling in parts—first her arms, then her chest, her legs, until even her feet were shimmying.

"Pull over, baby girl," Mom had said. "Before we get into an accident."

They'd sat in someone's driveway in silence for several long minutes.

"Let me drive home," her mother had said. And Gracelyn had walked woodenly to the passenger's seat and climbed in, adjusting the seat so that she was laying down, staring up at the fleecy beige ceiling.

"It'll all be okay," Mom had said. She'd dried her tears by then, wiped her face carefully with a tissue, straightened her shoulders. "There are still more tests to be done. Dr. Wolinsky might be wrong. And there are specialists..."

But Gracelyn wasn't listening anymore. She closed her eyes. This was what it would be like, she thought as she felt the car move back onto the road. This is what it would be like to live in darkness all the time. She kept her eyes clenched shut the rest of the ride home.

18

MACK COOLEY

SOUTHERN VERMONT

Nine Weeks Prior

"So this is where you grew up, huh?" Mack's voice tried and failed to hide disbelief. He slowed the car as they passed through the tiny town. Actually, "town" was giving it too much credit. The few buildings lining the main street were neglected-looking: paint peeling, sagging porches, roofs covered in moss and dead leaves left to rot on their surface. There were a handful of rusted cars and dented pickups lining the street. A couple of old men sitting on the steps of what Mack guessed to be the general store stared openly as Mack drove past. He raised a hand but they didn't wave back.

"This is it," Gracelyn responded, still staring out the window as she had been for the past forty minutes. "Paradise, huh?"

"It's not so bad," Mack tried to make his voice more neutral. "Quaint New England small town."

"Derelict wasteland is more like it."

Mack turned his head to look at Gracelyn and she glanced in his direction, then away, back out the window.

"Did you reach your family?"

Gracelyn nodded, then closed her eyes and let her head sink back onto the headrest. "You'll want to take the second left after the gas station. We'll cross a bridge and after that, you'll take a right. Then you'll see the farm."

Roger's farm was still humming along. Apparently her brother, unlike Gracelyn, had no desire to leave the little valley where the two had grown up. Her mother had moved in with him and his family shortly after Gracelyn's father had died. That's about all Mack knew about her family. He'd tried more than once to tease more information from her but was met with either disinterest or hostility, depending on Gracelyn's mood.

He'd come to love her over the past several months. Not only her determination and virtual boundless enthusiasm for life and adventure but her focus. Mack didn't appreciate wishy-washy and Gracelyn was the furthest thing from that he'd ever come across.

He cracked the window. The air was cold but refreshing. He breathed in, glanced automatically at the GPS. It was dark. No signal out this far, Gracelyn had told him and he'd turned it off miles back, wanting to save the battery. Besides, Gracelyn had reassured him, she could find her way home no matter what road they were on. Her sense of direction had been impressive in the woods. But in a moving car where Mack knew she couldn't see much of whatever landmarks they passed, it was truly remarkable.

"The bridge is just ahead. Careful, it's narrow. One car only really, though there's no sign to warn you of it," Gracelyn's voice sounded hollow. He glanced at her again then quickly back at the road. She was right, the road squeezed into itself like a tube of toothpaste and then spit them onto an old, metal bridge. The faded green paint was copper in some spots. Mack could make out initials and other graffiti splashed across its surface as they eased by.

Gracelyn hadn't been the same since they'd decided to come back here. They weren't staying—just on their way through to Maine where Mack had a summer rafting job lined up. Gracelyn had worked with a fishing company before and planned to ask if they needed any summer hands. If not, she was confident she could find something at a local state park or campground.

But since Mack had talked her into taking this side trip to visit her mother and brother on the way, she'd drawn into herself more and more. Over the past several months on the trail, they'd formed an easy bond. She'd become lighter and brighter than she had been even when they'd first met. Her friends—Jen and Nina—and moved on to the southwest. But Gracelyn had stayed behind. She and Mack had gone slowly and over time he'd been rewarded. Part of her shell had slipped off. There was still a lot of mystery and a lot she kept private, but he was confident she'd shared more of herself with him than she had anyone else in a long time.

The one thing she refused to talk about frequently was her father and the accident. She also rarely spoke of her family but when she did Mack was sure he'd recognized a note of longing there. That's why he'd been so adamant that they should stop by for a visit, however short.

Mack himself felt orphaned—his father had died when he was small and he'd been raised by his mother and her new husband, Neil. He and Mack had never seen eye-to-eye though and Mack had left home as soon as he'd graduated high school at seventeen. He still phoned his mother once a month but, didn't have much other contact. She was busy in the new life she'd created: they'd adopted a daughter from China the year after Mack left home. The three of them had a beautiful house in the suburbs of Chicago. Neil worked in the tech industry and for years had tried to convince Mack that making something of himself and getting a "real job" was what would make him happy. His mother agreed. Not because she necessarily felt the same way, but because she always agreed with Neil. It was the secret of their happy marriage.

"It's just ahead—the road—on your right," Gracelyn's voice interrupted Mack's thoughts. He loosened his hands on the steering wheel. He was a good one to be giving Gracelyn advice about her family, he thought and smiled sardonically.

The driveway to the farm was long and lined with potholes. The rental car bumped and bounced over its surface, no matter how slowly Mack went. A black and white dog started barking as they approached the yard, but his furiously wagging tail made Mack smile. Gracelyn had had a dog, Trek, she'd told him. Mack would like to get one someday—had loved the one they'd had when he was young—but his transient lifestyle made it difficult.

"Here we are," he said, more to fill up the silent space in the car's interior than to share any surprising news.

Gracelyn didn't move. Her eyes remained closed, her head continued to rest against the seat. He'd have thought she was sleeping if she hadn't been giving directions seconds before.

"What's the pooch's name?" he asked, edging the car onto the side of the driveway and turning off the ignition.

"I don't know." Gracelyn's voice was so quiet Mack could

barely hear it. Then, "This was a mistake. Mack, I don't want
to do this. I don't—"

"Someone's coming out of the shed near the barn. Tall
guy, big belly, dark hair."

"Roger."

Mack waved through the windshield. "Come on. It's too
late to turn around now, he's on his way over."

Gracelyn remained immobile.

"Suit yourself," Mack said and climbed out from behind
the wheel. The dog yipped and jumped around as though it
was on a bed of red ants.

Roger approached, wiping his hands on a bandana that
had once been red. "Afternoon," he said, his voice surprisingly melodic. "Can I help you?"

Before Mack could answer, Roger said, "Piper, down."
The dog stopped jumping but kept circling, wagging its tail.

Mack walked toward Roger, hand outstretched. Roger
took his hand in a firm, calloused grip.

"I'm Mack Cooley. Gracelyn's friend." He nodded toward
the car.

All the color in Roger's cheeks drained away and he
stared at the car. His hand had turned limp in Mack's. Mack
let it slide from his own and glanced toward the house when
the front door opened. A woman who could have been
Gracelyn's twin emerged. She had graying hair and fine lines
around her eyes and mouth, but other than that looked
unnervingly like her daughter. She perched on the steps.

"Hello," Mack called and waved. The woman raised her
hand in a stiff wave, her eyes flicking between Mack, Roger,
and the car.

The passenger door opened and Gracelyn slipped out.
She too looked pale but forced a smile onto her face.

"Roger. Mom. I'm home."

"I JUST DON'T GET why you lied and said you'd told them you were coming—we were coming—when you hadn't," Mack said, trying to keep his voice level. It was late at night. Roger and Emily—Gracelyn's mother insisted he call her by her first name—had gone to bed hours ago.

"Farmers' hours," Roger had said with a slow grin. Mack liked him and told Gracelyn so. "He's easy to get along with," Mack had said. "He doesn't talk a lot but thinks before he speaks."

Gracelyn had only nodded mutely.

Now, she reached over the arm of her chair and squeezed his hand. Her fingers were dry and warm despite the cold, wet weather outdoors. A thunderstorm had moved in shortly after they'd arrived and the temperature had dropped rapidly.

"I didn't not tell them. I just didn't give them a specific date."

"I think your mom said you'd mentioned you 'might be coming in the next several months,' the last time she talked to you."

"Yeah," Gracelyn said and yawned. "That sounds about right."

"But that was only a couple of weeks ago. Before we left Colorado."

"What do you want me to say, Mack? I didn't want to give them a firm date because then I'd be wedded to it, okay? And honestly, I wasn't sure I could do this. Could be here again. I was leaving myself an out."

She pulled her hand away or tried to, but he held on tighter.

"It's fine. I was just surprised, I guess." He massaged her palm and she relaxed slightly.

"I need sleep," she said, but didn't move away from the fireplace.

"Your mom asked me how long we were planning to stay. I told her until Thursday. That's still the plan isn't it?"

Gracelyn shrugged. "Sure," she said. "I guess that's still the plan."

"All right. I'd better head up. I'm going to help Roger in the morning with the milking."

Gracelyn burst into a peal of laughter and then clapped a hand over her mouth. "You aren't serious."

"Hey, when in Rome..." Mack let his voice drift.

"You're crazy. Don't get kicked."

"Kicked? Cows kick?"

"Sometimes." Gracelyn yawned again and stretched her arms up over her head. "If you aren't gentle enough when you're milking." She stood, the afghan that had been over her knees fell to the floor.

"But I'm sure you'll be fine," she said. "You've got very gentle hands."

Mack chuckled and stood up too. He wrapped his arms around Gracelyn's waist. She responded by sinking her face into his neck. She smelled good. Like cedar and roses mixed together. He could feel her pulse under her earlobe and kissed the spot.

She shifted slightly, pressed herself closer to him.

"Now, Mr. Cooley. Hired hands don't get to have relations with the womenfolk here on the farm."

"Oh, no?" He smiled as he kissed a line down her neck

and into her collarbone. "Well then, it's a good thing I'm not getting paid for this farm work."

Gracelyn chuckled and began to kiss his cheek which he knew was rough and scratchy.

"You didn't get the rest of the tour earlier, did you?" she asked and tugged him along behind her. "I think you'll be especially interested in my old bedroom."

19

GRACELYN EDWARDS

THE TUNNEL, DIABLO POINT

Present Day

Gracelyn wasn't sure how long she'd stood in the entrance of the tunnel, processing the information that Mack was gone and so was the snake.

She turned in the tunnel, once, twice, looking for anything that would give her a clue as to where they'd gone. Moving close to the tunnel walls, she felt along them—first one side and then the other—but found nothing other than crumbly dirt and the occasional embedded stone. She poked around the ground, shining her flashlight over it. It was too blurry for her to really get a good look, so she went down on hands and knees again, looking for any sign of Mack. Her hands explored small crevices and rounded stones poking out of the dirt. Her palms scraped over rough, more jagged rocks and twice she felt the unpleasant squish of a slug under her as she moved over the floor of the tunnel.

She was almost at the entrance when she found it. Mack's jackknife. He always had it in his right-hand pocket. She fingered it, brought it closer to her face and shone the light beam directly at it. But there was no other clue there. No blood. No hidden message penned in a frantic hand in the tunnel wall. She smiled wryly and tucked the knife into her own pocket. Still. It was proof that Mack had come this way, or been pulled along here.

But why?

Gracelyn stood in the entrance of the tunnel now, blinking against the sudden too-bright light of the sun. Her eyes watered and she wiped the back of her hand over them. Why wouldn't it have killed him—and her—right here in the tunnel? And where would it have taken him instead?

An old, very deep shame coated Gracelyn's belly like a thick, sludgy film. She'd done this to Mack. He was missing because of her, just like she'd left her father here, alone to die. It was her fault Dad was dead. Tears threatened to spill and she wiped at her eyes angrily.

If she was going to save Mack she had to deal with facts not feelings. Feelings were going to get them both killed out here. She'd had enough near-fatal experiences in her years of hiking to know that panic and giving in to your feelings was the worst thing to do in a precarious position.

Think. Think. What's different this time than the last?

The most obvious thing was that rather than pulling Mack back into the rear of the cave, where it seemed the snake liked to store its food, it had pulled him out of the front. Why would it do that?

Gracelyn bit her lip and paced the floor in a tight, cramped circle. Because it had a second lair. Perhaps a place where it stored more of its prey. But why? Why two? Most snakes in nature had only one and even those weren't normally created by the snakes themselves. They usually took over an existing tunnel made by a chipmunk or some other small animal. But not this one. There wasn't an animal that Gracelyn could think of large enough to dig out a tunnel-like this.

She frowned. The more she thought about it, the farther the snake could be going with Mack. It had to be moving more slowly. Mack wasn't a big guy but the snake would be awkwardly carrying or dragging an extra one hundred and seventy-ish pounds. It couldn't be taking him far.

She put a hand over her forehead and squeezed. She wanted to retrace her steps, get their packs and then go look for Mack. But the other part of her knew that was foolish. She'd lose precious time. Mack could be taken so far away that she'd never—

She stopped herself. She was going to find him. No matter what. Gracelyn shifted forward and climbed out the front of the tunnel. She turned the flashlight off and pocketed it. That along with the pistol in her waistband made her pants droop slightly. She felt around the outside of the tunnel and tried to remember how she'd first scaled the slippery pieces of shale when she'd been here before. Breaking off a young sapling took a few precious minutes that she didn't have, but it would be worth it. Digging it into the sliding stones underfoot helped to ground her and keep her more stable.

Gracelyn looked around the woods beneath her. The trees were sparse, the ground black with shale. But further down there was tree cover and low-lying bushes, easy for the snake to hide in. She pushed herself into a crouching position and began to half crabwalk, half slide down the face of the summit.

GRACELYN'S MOUTH FELT GUMMY. She tried to draw saliva up from her throat, but it didn't work. She'd been moving for over forty minutes, following the tangled trail first, thinking the snake would choose it because it offered the least resistance. But by now Gracelyn was starting to question every decision she'd made since leaving the tunnel.

Had she gone the right direction? Had she been foolish to leave the packs behind? What was she going to do out here when it got dark?

Shoving the thoughts away, she dug her makeshift walking stick into the undergrowth and paused in her descent. She leaned against a tree trunk and listened. The forest—like any place—had its own rhythm, its own soundtrack. If she attuned herself to it perhaps it could help lead her to the snake.

She heard nothing for several long seconds, other than the squeak overhead of two branches rubbing together. Gracelyn frowned and listened harder. No, still nothing. And then she realized that the lack of noise was telling her a story of its own. Normally the woods were alive with sound during the day: birds chattering and bickering about territory overhead; small chipmunks and squirrels rummaging around through the dead leaves and fallen branches on the ground; even the sound of insects filling the air with buzzes and whines and chirps.

But not here. Everything around her was still and silent. Because of the snake. The animals must sense its presence. She closed her eyes and listened harder. Far, far away she could just make out the soft drone of an airplane in the western edge of the sky. The branches ahead squeaked once more.

And then she heard something else. Faintly, so faint that at first she dismissed it. But the soft sound continued and Gracelyn strained her ears to hear it. It sounded like leaves when they blew over wet grass. The soft swish of dryness over something not as dry.

Gracelyn focused every bit of her attention on the sound. It was the snake. It had to be it, moving over the ground, its thick, scaled body sinuously gliding over the earth. Where was it coming from? Gracelyn's heartbeat had increased and it too filled her ears. She took a couple of deep breaths, trying to quiet the loud throb in her ears. For a few precious seconds, she thought she'd lost the sound completely. But then she heard it again, faintly—even more faintly than before—and turned her face in the direction of the sound.

It was coming from above her and slightly to the left. Across from the summit of Diablo Peak—the tunnel that she and Mack had come from—was another, smaller mountain. She opened her eyes and started to move in that direction. Gracelyn strained to see signs of the snake or Mack but even a fully seeing person likely wouldn't be able to detect them in the thick undergrowth.

After stumbling twice and nearly falling another time, Gracelyn closed her eyes and put out her hands. The blurry landscape turned completely dark but her ears picked up the sound of the snake's movements again. She attuned her ears to it, blocking out everything else and moved slowly, gropingly into the woods.

20

EMILY EDWARDS

SOUTHERN VERMONT

Nine Weeks Prior

E mily stirred her tea and looked into the mug as though hoping to find answers there. She knew it was futile. Answers were elusive where her daughter was concerned. If someone had told Emily after she'd had Roger—such an easy, sweet baby to love—that she'd have had a colicky, stubborn, willful child like Gracelyn, she wouldn't have believed them. She'd thought all babies came wrapped in sweet-cheeked packages. But Gracelyn's iron will and stubbornness didn't fade as she grew out of toddlerhood. Instead, it had grown in proportion. Like the faded measuring wall by the back door, Gracelyn's independence that bordered on foolishness had kept pace with the little tick marks that showed her height increases. And it had only gotten worse when she'd lost her eyesight.

Shawn used to tell Emily that she was too hard on

Gracelyn. That she needed to stop trying to make Gracie into a mini Emily or another Roger. But honestly? Emily had felt as though her own daughter were an alien being, plopped into their family.

Where Emily and Shawn and Roger were all laid back and easygoing, Gracelyn was fiery and confrontational. Shawn had loved that about her, giving her the nickname "Spitfire" when she was two. The name had stuck throughout her childhood.

"You need to just accept her for who she is," Shawn had told Emily over and over when she'd gripe about some new problem with Gracelyn. "And watch for what she can teach you."

Oh yes, thought Emily grimly now as she sipped her lukewarm tea. Her daughter had taught her a lot in the past couple of years.

The floorboards overhead creaked and Emily heard soft footfalls as someone descended the stairs. Moments later a mop of wayward curls made its way around the corner into the kitchen.

"Good morning," Mack said with a slow smile showing off very white teeth. He looked at her shyly almost and she couldn't help but smile back.

"Morning," she said. "There's a kettle on if you want tea. Coffee's just about done brewing. Roger's already out."

"Thanks. Coffee sounds great. Where will I find the mugs?"

Emily stood and ushered him to the table. "I'll get that for you. We usually have breakfast after morning chores. It's too time-consuming beforehand. Plus, Roger likes to eat with the kids."

"The twins?"

Emily nodded. Gracelyn and Mack had seen her three-year-old granddaughters briefly before they'd been bundled into their car for an overnight at their grandparents' house. Emily thought of her daughter-in-law's parents with a mixture of guilt and affection. Guilt because she never felt like she measured up. Affection because despite their wealth, they'd never once been unkind or made Emily or Roger feel "less than". Indeed, they'd gone out of their way to support Roger and Emily financially after Shawn's death, before the life insurance policy had kicked in. And they hadn't allowed the money to be repaid. Emily would be eternally grateful.

"So, Gracelyn said you'll be working as a river tour guide in Maine?" Emily asked as she set the mug of steaming coffee in front of Mack. He nodded as he stirred in fresh cream, no sugar.

"Yeah, it's a pretty good gig. I've worked there before—a few summers ago—and had a good time. It pays well, too. Well, you know, for that type of work."

Mack glanced at her. Was he embarrassed because he didn't feel like he could provide for Gracelyn? Emily was touched by his chivalry, however misplaced.

"And Gracie is planning to work at a state park?"

"I think she said she wants to try the fishing company first. But if it doesn't pan out then that's her backup plan," Mack said and sipped from his mug. "Good coffee, thank you."

Emily just nodded. "Mack, I know that we've barely met and this question might seem intrusive. But I have to ask it anyway: how much do you know about Gracelyn's father's death?"

Mack stopped with the mug halfway to the table.

"Not much." He set the cup down gently. "She doesn't like to talk about it."

Emily sighed and leaned back in her chair. "I'm not sure if this is my place. If I should tell you this or wait for Gracelyn to do it herself. But knowing Gracelyn that might be in about two decades or more."

Mack smiled.

Emily pressed her lips together. Who knew when they'd have time together alone again?

"Shawn and Gracie were always close. Even through the traumatic teen years, he was the one person whom she really had a good bond with. Sure, they disagreed on things. Well, mostly Gracelyn disagreed with Shawn."

"Sounds about right," Mack said.

Emily smiled. "But he would always encourage her to share her point of view with him. Always try to get her to explain *why* she felt the way she did. It became a sort of running joke between them—him playing investigator to her strong feelings.

"But oftentimes I felt that he gave Gracelyn too much power. Too much control. She was already headstrong and stubborn—she came out of the womb that way—and Shawn and I differed in how to best handle that. I guess that's one of the reasons that Gracelyn and I have never been close."

Emily shook her head. "Anyway. What I wanted to tell you is that Shawn died as a result of something Gracelyn wanted. He had a phobia of snakes, but Gracelyn was on a mission to investigate the supposed huge serpent that lives up on Diablo Point. It's an old folktale, handed down by who knows how many generations. Gracelyn was writing a blog about monsters and folklore and doing what she called, 'investigative journalism.'" Emily made air quotes with her fingers. "Shawn agreed to go with her up there, to see if they could find it." Emily pushed her mug away and then pulled it close again. "Gracelyn came home from that adventure, but Shawn didn't."

The grandfather clock ticked in the hallway and outside a cow mooed as Roger opened the barn up for the day.

"I'm not saying that it was Gracelyn's fault. I just..." her voice faded away and she traced a whorl in the wood on the battered kitchen table. "I'm just saying please be careful. Gracie has a way of talking some people into doing things against their better judgment. Shawn was one of those people. What's that old saying? 'Love is blind'? Well, it can be. And I'd hate to see anything—"

"What's that, Mom? Warning Mack that I might get him killed too?"

Gracelyn's voice cut through the quiet room. Emily jumped, jerked her gaze to the kitchen door where Gracelyn stood, half in and half out of the room. Her body trembled. She had her arms wrapped around her and her chin jutted out.

"Gracie. I—"

"Save it." Gracelyn spat the words out. "I cannot believe you. I'm not even home a day and you're already at it. When are you going to stop blaming me? It wasn't my fault! I didn't know Dad was afraid of snakes. I didn't know what was going to happen up there, okay?"

Mack stood and crossed the room to Gracelyn. She put her hands up as though to fend him off.

"I'm done here."

"I didn't mean that," Emily said and she too stood. "I didn't mean that it was your fault. Please just—"

"I'll be in the car in twenty minutes," Gracelyn said to Mack. "If you don't want to leave with me—"

"Wait, hold on a second. I think we should all back up a step and calm down. Your mother didn't mean—"

"I know what she meant. And so does she." Gracelyn's voice was hollow. "Twenty minutes. I'll hitchhike if you don't want to take me."

"No, please don't—" Emily tried again. But she was talking to an empty doorway.

"I'm sorry," she said to Mack. He still stood there facing the doorway, his hands held up like he was still holding Gracelyn's.

"It's all right," Mack said. "I...she and I haven't talked much about that..." his voice cut out for a second. "That day."

"And now I've gone and made a mess of it." Emily shook her head. "Once again, it's Gracelyn one point, me zero." She smiled but it took effort. "Let me pack up a little something for the road. It's early and the diner in town won't be open for breakfast yet."

"That's okay," Mack said. "I'm sorry that I won't get to play farmhand for the day."

Emily smiled but it didn't reach her eyes. "Roger will be sorry too."

"Next time, huh?" Mack said. He looked about to follow Gracelyn's path from the room, but then stopped and crossed the distance to Emily. He leaned down and hugged her gently. Tears sprang to Emily's eyes. She blinked them away hard.

"Where will you go now?"

"I'm not sure," Mack said, drawing back. "But thank you for your hospitality. And I'll keep working on her. She might change her mind in a day or two, you never know."

Emily made an agreeing sound but didn't believe him. She did know. She knew her daughter better than Gracie knew herself.

In the end, Emily had been surprised. She didn't know how, but Mack had talked Gracelyn into staying for the rest of the week. They'd camp at the local state park rather than stay at the house, but it was a good compromise. When they visited, Gracelyn was lovable with the twins who followed her around, asking for horsey rides and stories about her adventures. Their mother, Sadie, took Gracelyn out for a "girl's day" shopping in the larger city of Rutland an hour and a half away. She'd treated her to lunch and a salt cave treatment that Sadie loved and Gracelyn tolerated.

And then the day they were supposed to leave: Mack got a call telling him that due to flooding, the river rafting season was being postponed. So he'd picked up some work with a road crew and Gracelyn had found a temporary job at the local nature preserve giving tours of the wetlands and the animals that lived there.

They'd stayed two more months than they were planning. And when it came time for them to leave, there had been a big fight. Not between Gracelyn and Emily this time though, but Mack and Gracelyn. Emily had caught the tail end of it, coming in from the garden in time to hear a plate smash and Gracelyn insisting that she "wanted to be left alone".

Emily had no idea then what the fight was about. Or that Gracelyn would soon find herself again climbing Diablo Point, looking for the snake that she believed was responsible for Shawn's death.

21

GRACELYN EDWARDS

THE TUNNEL, DIABLO POINT

Present Day

The sound of the snake's body moving over the undergrowth grew louder. Gracelyn's dry throat made her want to cough but she held it in. Her lips were cracked when she licked them. Scaling a dead tree, its bark pliable and crumbly under her hands, something squishy wriggled under her palm.

The sound of the snake was louder. That meant Gracelyn's movements had to be even quieter. If it knew she was following...

Clouds must have covered the sun because her skin felt suddenly chilly. She swallowed again and then heard it.

A groan.

A man's groan.

Mack.

Everything in Gracelyn wanted to hurry, to speed up. Instead, she forced herself to slow her pace. She had to find out where the snake was taking Mack before she could save him.

Then another sound came from overhead and to her right. Gracelyn opened her eyes and looked in that direction. She swept the landscape above her. There was an outcropping of large rocks, half-buried in dirt and moss. Along the side closest to where Gracelyn stood was a stone overhang. It was large enough for some animal or person to hide in. Could that be where the snake entered a second tunnel? But no, Gracelyn looked from the rocks to the summit above her. The snake was there, still climbing its way upward. The thick vegetation prevented her from seeing well, but she could just make out movement in the undergrowth and a glimpse of the red shirt Mack was wearing.

There! The sound came again from her right. She looked back just in time to see a pair of eyes watching her. They were bright flashes in the dark of the shadowed ledge. She couldn't make out anything else. Was it a raccoon or fisher cat? No. Something larger.

Gracelyn's heartbeat galloped fast in her chest. A line of cold sweat beaded against her backbone. She slowly reached behind her back and pulled the gun free. Keeping it at her leg and her gaze toward the stone overhang, she walked sideways up the mountain. It was cumbersome and slow going and she was afraid she'd lose the snake completely. But Gracelyn wasn't about to become lunch for whatever it was hiding in the rocks. She glanced toward the snake and swore. It was gaining ground. She glanced behind her and whatever animal was hiding in the rocks.

A sudden noise above her jerked Gracelyn's attention back. The snake had disappeared. In its wake was the sound of stones clinking together. Then a low, quiet hiss filled the air. Panicked, Gracelyn ran forward toward where she'd last seen Mack. Her arms pumped, her hand was sweaty on the Ruger's grip. She panted and tried to stop. She needed to hear if that thing—whatever it was—was coming behind her. She imagined a shaggy beast—a bear, a coyote— launching itself out of the dark woods and onto her body.

Her breath was loud in her ears. The only other thing she could hear in the silent forest was the sound of her heart, like a drumbeat in her head.

The hiss of the snake was fainter. She must be almost to where Mack was. Why had the snake left him? She tripped on a root and nearly fell. Caught herself on a tree's trunk and kept running. She didn't bother trying to be quiet anymore. She just ran.

Something watched her. She looked around her wildly but couldn't make anything out among the blurred trees and bushes. She stopped abruptly, hid behind a large, tangled swatch of thorn bushes. She watched. From behind her, where she'd just been running, a shadow moved along the ground. It was large and feline. A mountain cat? She'd thought those had all died out. Gracelyn put a hand over her mouth, trying to quiet her too-loud breath.

Then, before she could even understand what happened, the giant snake shot out from the ground above her. There was a hole in the side of the mountain, larger than on Diablo Peak. The dark serpentine body flew out of it, sailing through the air. It can fly, Gracelyn thought, before the snake hurtled to the ground and wrapped itself around the animal that had been following Gracelyn.

She stood from her crouch, her legs screaming. Gracelyn looked in horror as the huge body of the snake wrapped itself around a mountain lion. The catamount had a golden body that writhed now in the snake's grip.

Get to Mack.

Now was the only chance Gracelyn might have. The catamount screamed in agony as it twisted in the gruesome embrace of the serpent. Gracelyn plowed upward toward the tunnel in the side of the second mountain.

Her legs were jelly, her body coated in sweat. She ran harder, shoving aside low-hanging branches that slapped back into her face and tore at her clothes and hair. A moan came from the mountain lion behind her, but it was softer now. More a gasping plea than the earlier howls of surprise and pain.

Gracelyn saw movement from the opening in the side of the mountain. Mack? Was the venom wearing off? Perhaps its paralyzing effect only lasted a short time. Maybe that's why the snake was moving him to this second tunnel. It might stun its prey and then bring it here for safekeeping. But why?

The tunnel mouth gaped in front of her. A shadow shifted inside of the black hole. Gracelyn assumed it was sunbeams moving over the opening. Another thought quickly followed: maybe this snake had a partner. Goosebumps rose on Gracelyn's sweaty skin.

She stopped. Squinted. Her heart ground to a halt before smashing into her chest again ten times faster. Behind the opening was another set of eyes. No, Gracelyn realized with horror. More than one. One there, a second to the left. Further back another pair shone in the dim light of the cavern's entrance. Three. Three more snakes. Smaller. Juvenile? Their bodies were wide but slender compared to the huge one she'd seen before. They bobbed their heads, rippling in place like they were dancing to unheard music.

One of the smaller snakes started to wriggle toward the opening of the cave. Another nearby, bigger and darker, lunged toward it, snapping its jaws and rows of teeth—like a shark's—in front of the smaller one's face. The smaller one shrank back silently into the darkness.

Gracelyn stood and swallowed away the rancid taste of fear. Lying half inside, half outside the tunnel was Mack. Curled on his side. Immobile. The adult snake—the mother —had left her children lunch while she went to kill dessert. Gracelyn stared in disbelief as the largest of the three juveniles rear its head back. Its sharp teeth glinted in the sunlight as it prepared to tear into Mack's prone form.

"When you get ready to shoot, do it in three simple steps," Roger had told her. They'd worked together for hours in a field far from where the cows grazed. Gracelyn could hear his voice counting out the steps.

One: she jerked her hand upright.

Two: she clamped both of her hands around the gun's grip.

Three: she fired.

22

EMILY EDWARDS

SOUTHERN VERMONT

Three Days Prior

The morning of the fight between Gracelyn and Mack, Emily had woken with a bitter taste in her mouth. It lasted through her morning tea and early chores. She'd lived in Bondville long enough to recognize the signs that things weren't right. All wasn't as it ought to be.

Bondville was little more than a tiny collection of miscellaneous people. Like a jigsaw puzzle missing too many pieces to ever be put together correctly. The town had been formed generations before by two groups of people: those like Shawn's ancestors who'd come from Salem to escape the witch hunt madness and the misfits—the oddball characters who'd lived on the fringes and liked it that way. In the little raggle-taggle town there was an unspoken agreement: live and let live. Minding your own business was a given.

Through the years Shawn's family—like every other one in the area—had been laced with the folklore of the place. Supposed devil worshipers nearby in The Settlement. A creature higher up in the further away mountains near Glaston who sounded suspiciously like Bigfoot. And a serpent larger than any Vermont snake had a right to be, which lived in a tunnel at the top of Diablo Point.

Emily, having moved here at age fourteen, had never believed the stories. They were invented for entertainment. They'd provided hours of it during the long and very dull winters before television came along, she thought. But Shawn had believed in them. Some of the others in Bondville did too. Those who believed fell into two camps: they'd lived here the longest and they spent the most time in the woods.

Shawn had told Emily stories about the giant snake some late evenings, after a few glasses of scotch. She remembered his face, the look on it somewhere between curiosity and fear as he'd stared into the flickering flames of the woodstove.

Emily had grown up in Brattleboro and had only moved here after her parents had caught the "back to the land" fever. Unable to afford a farm where they were living, they'd moved their family to Bondville. They'd had high hopes of finding a land flowing with milk, honey, and opportunities. Instead, they'd discovered stress and hardship and failure and moved back to the city. By then though, Emily was eighteen and had fallen in love with both Shawn and the beautiful, rugged land. She'd never left.

She took another deep drink of water and stared unseeingly out of the square window over the kitchen sink. Sadie and the girls were at a playgroup and Roger was working out in the lower fields, fixing a fence with the hired man. She'd been in the garden until a few minutes ago.

Now, her hip pressed painfully into the counter, but she didn't move. Her thoughts turned to the tail end of the fight she'd interrupted between Gracelyn and Mack. Words between them since had been few and hard-edged.

It wasn't unusual for Gracelyn to have a difference of opinion with Mack or anyone else. But Emily knew that this had been something else. Something more. A sort of breaking that Emily could almost hear in the silence between them, like a butter dish crashing to the floor or a china platter snapping in two. There was a finality to the silence. Or maybe, Emily smiled and put her empty glass in the sink, she was just being silly.

$\sim$

Two Days Prior

EMILY WISHED she had been wrong. Wrong about the finality of the fight between her daughter and Mack. Wrong about where she suspected Emily had gone when Roger had taken his sister on an impromptu drive this morning. Wrong about everything.

She pressed her lips together and wrapped her arms around her middle. The rocker under her moved as though on its own and she let herself be hypnotized by its comforting embrace. Every third rock one of the gliders groaned. *Rock-rock-squeak, rock-rock-squeak.*

Roger would be back soon and Emily was going to get the truth from him, no matter what. She heard Sadie and the girls through the open windows of the farmhouse. There was the clink of glass and the sound of something being stirred in a pot. If the girls knew Emily was out here, they'd tumble out the door, hair sticking up, books in hands, ready to climb into her lap and let Nana read them as many stories as possible before her throat grew sore.

She smiled at the thought of the girls. She was so lucky to have them in her life—a light that shone after the long, dark days of Shawn... Emily blinked her eyes quickly and looked back at the book in her lap. Her mother's Bible, handed down to Emily before Mother had succumbed to cancer all those years back. Emily hadn't cracked it open in years. She'd never felt the need and was too busy dealing with both her grief and her ailing father's health to spend time chatting with God about her problems. Besides. If he'd cared so much, why had he just sat there, letting her mother go through so much pain?

But after Shawn died something in Emily had too. She'd gone into a dark place, so dark she knew she should have been afraid that she'd never come out. The thing was—she didn't care if she did or not. Life, which she'd pictured a certain way, had come undone. Without Shawn, Emily saw only days and months and years to be filled with...what? They stood before her, empty and bleak. And she didn't want to face them alone.

It was a chance meeting with an old friend who'd also recently lost her own husband that had put a question in Emily's mind.

"How do you cope?" Emily had asked over robust coffee at a local café in Wilmington. "How do you go on day after day without him?"

Nancy had smiled and laid a warm, soft hand over Emily's own. "It gets easier, a little at a time. The days don't

—they don't move in an upward direction the way we'd like —but over the months you start to see that there is purpose again, that there is meaning. At least I did. But then, I have my faith—"

"What faith?" Emily had asked, grasping like a drowning woman at any shred of hope.

"In God," Nancy had responded. "In goodness and light. That's what it all comes down to, isn't it? A belief that there is something more than us. That there is someone bigger than us and our problems."

"That's what you cling to?" Emily had asked. "What if you're wrong?"

"What, about the afterlife? Heaven and all of that?"

Emily had nodded. Heaven to her had always been a fairy tale told in Sunday school classes to pudgy-fingered toddlers who hadn't been exposed to the harsh reality of life.

"The thought brings comfort, yes," Nancy had said. "But I'd live this way even if there weren't a promise of anything after death."

"Why?" Emily had asked, unable to keep the incredulity out of her voice. "It seems like such a drag. Always worrying about doing the right or wrong things. Always feeling pressured that there's some giant entity watching you screw up and taking notes." She hadn't meant for her voice to sound so bitter, but honestly, this was Nancy's comforting answer? That she believed in God?

Emily wanted real, practical advice for doing the daily tasks that drained her: getting dressed, eating, brushing her teeth, responding to her family's questions with semi-intelligent answers. Today—this venture into the pretty little town had taken so much effort. Emily needed real answers: when her heart would stop literally aching in her chest? Would she ever laugh again? Why had Shawn been taken instead of her?

"Because my faith brings me comfort," Nancy had said. "Not just the thought of a far-away, magical place after I die. That's great, but it's this life that makes me need my faith to cope. To survive. I don't think I'm explaining it very well," Nancy had laughed. "But does it make any sense to you?"

"Mmm," Emily had said unconvinced. She'd stirred her coffee unnecessarily and changed the subject.

But she couldn't get Nancy's words out of her mind. "I'd live this way even if there weren't a promise of anything after death." And so, days later, Emily had dug her mother's old Bible with its black leather cover out of the attic and started reading it.

She wasn't sure what she was reading half the time but something strange started to happen. She was finding peace within the pages of the old book. Sometimes she looked for answers and most of the time she didn't find any specific suggestions. But often words or phrases stood out on the page like they were written there just for her. It was an odd, unnerving experience but it also brought her peace. And those few moments of peace made returning to the book, again and again, a regular part of Emily's day.

Would it lead anywhere further? She didn't know. And it didn't really matter, did it? What mattered was that the practice was giving her peace—a small measure of it—and she would take any of that she could get.

Now, Emily closed the big book and let her mind drift. She knew what she needed to do if Roger told her that he'd taken Gracelyn where Emily suspected he had. She knew too, that she couldn't let her family know where she was going. They would try to stop her. It would upset the twins and leave Roger and Sadie feeling helpless—and what was the point of that? But if Roger had brought Gracelyn to Diablo Point this morning, then Emily was going after her.

Dust rose in the distance and Emily stood up, setting the Bible down in the empty chair. She could just make out Roger's battered Ford headed toward the house. Emily walked across the porch and down the stairs and waited.

23

GRACELYN EDWARDS

DIABLO POINT TRAIL

Present Day

The shot missed.

Whereas Gracelyn had been expecting to blow the snake's head into two ragged pieces, the slug had instead hit the wall too far to its right. She was too far away. The blast had been thunderous and her ears were ringing. She rushed forward, toward Mack. Rather than sliding away in fear as she'd expected, the three snakes moved closer to the opening of the tunnel.

Gracelyn pushed herself faster toward them.

Hurry. Hurry!

Noise was coming from below her—the mother snake?—and Gracelyn gasped as she leaped over a rotten stump. She was almost there. She kept the Ruger in her hand, its grip rough against her clammy palm. She bent low, the steep incline forcing her to crabwalk toward the last of the bushes that separated her from him.

"Mack?" she cried. He looked all wrong. His body was stiff and frozen looking like rigor mortis had already set in.

"Mack!" she screamed again. It didn't matter anymore if the snakes heard her.

A hissing sound came from above. Gracelyn jerked toward it. The second snake—the smaller one that had been trying to come out earlier—flicked its tongue. It lunged forward so quickly she barely had time to think. She squeezed the trigger again. This time she didn't miss. The snake's head crumpled and bits of fibrous tissue and bloodied muscle rained down on her and Mack. Gracelyn's ears ached as she straightened her arm, got ready to take another shot.

She never made it.

Instead, the largest of the three juveniles reared back its head and plunged forward, driving its jagged teeth into Mack's chest and neck. Blood spurted upward. There was a horrible gurgling sound. The coppery scent of blood and other fleshy smells filled the air. Gracelyn gagged.

"No!" she cried. "Mack—"

The third snake—the medium-sized one—was drawing close. Gracelyn barely recognized it. She shot again, wildly, barely bothering to take aim. Tears blurred her vision and she howled. She fired. One shot went off, then another and another. The remaining snakes drew back momentarily. But when the Ruger was out of bullets and the only thing that remained was the impotent *click, click, click* when she pressed the trigger, they resumed their places.

A dull coldness had fallen over Gracelyn's body. It was like that thick, heavy apron they make you wear at the dentist when they take X-rays. She knew she was in danger. But she didn't care.

Mack.

A funny sound was coming from somewhere nearby, partway between a gasping whine and a howl. Oh, Gracelyn thought, it's coming from me. Still, she didn't move. The snakes had surrounded Mack, both taking turns dipping their heads down toward his body and then coming back up, with pieces of his shirt, his flesh in their mouths...

Gracelyn slipped and let herself fall backward. The gun fell from her hand and she heard it bounce downward. Another sound filled the dulled echo in her ears: the sound of the big snake coming back.

She should be afraid. She should run. She should try to save herself.

Instead, she lay on the ground, looking up at the canopy of bright-green leaves overhead. They shook and danced in a breeze she couldn't see. She felt rather than saw the shape of the mother snake over her. Mother. Was it a mother? Or the father? Either way, Gracelyn had killed at least one of its young.

But it had taken two of the people Gracelyn had loved most.

A strange hissing filled the air, deep and low, like air leaking from a massive tire. Seconds later, two higher-pitched hisses responded. Gracelyn saw the snake's head now. It loomed above her.

Go ahead. Take me too.

Her brain and body dull, Gracelyn waited.

And then pain, like someone had thrown acid onto her skin, seared her right ribcage. She cried out in spite of herself, then curled onto her side instinctively protecting the spot. Fiery heat crept outward from the spot. A deadening coldness followed.

Gracelyn could barely breathe. Gasping, she lay prone on the forest floor.

Let it happen quickly. Let me die now.

Mack's red flannel shirt was the last thing she saw before the world around her went dark.

GRACELYN COULD HEAR fragments of voices around her but everything was black and still. She heard her father laughing at something, then Roger's voice gruff and low. She didn't know why, but it felt like they were at a picnic, maybe at the lake. The twins squealed and then her mother's voice responded to them. Gracelyn heard water lapping at the shore. Mack's low timber murmured something she couldn't quite make out. Gracelyn smiled in response.

What had it been though? She thought hard, trying to remember but it was gone. And then the voices were gone too. Replaced by the sound of wind moving in the trees and water rushing. Then the sound of something heavy sliding over something rough, the occasional bumps and thumps jarring her body. Then the sound of nothing.

24

EMILY EDWARDS

DIABLO POINT TRAIL

Present Day

Emily frowned and checked the map again. She'd found it in Shawn's "office" the term they'd used loosely to describe the hodge-podge room that he'd kept at the back of the house. When the kids were small it had been the nursery, but over the years more and more of Shawn's things had appeared in the room until finally, Emily had offered to help him paint it and move out the last of the baby furniture. He'd insisted it hadn't needed painting—the sage green walls were fine—but had accepted her help in rehoming the crib, small bureau and rocking chair to the attic.

Now, she squinted at the map, tracing the line over and over again with her finger. She did not want to get lost out here. GPS units didn't work and she had no idea where she was going. She pulled the compass out of her pocket and double checked it again. It had been ages since she'd last used a compass and map—maybe since the orienteering class she'd taken with Shawn before the kids had come along.

Emily bit her lip and looked at the woods ahead of her. They were twisted and dark. The branches seemed to pull away from tree trunks just to reach for her. Vines hung here and there, smothering other trees and blocking out the light. Still, she was fairly confident this was the right way.

She'd hoped to see some signs of Gracelyn and Mack— maybe footprints, some stray hairs caught on a branch or bits of wrappers that the wind had taken. There was nothing. Gracelyn was meticulous about making sure nothing got left behind, so Emily shouldn't be surprised. Her daughter had once yelled at another hiker when she was only twelve, chastising the thirty-something-year-old for leaving behind the wrapping from his sandwich. Emily had been mortified; Shawn had been proud.

The pack dug into her shoulders and she adjusted the straps, trying to alleviate the discomfort. It didn't help. Emily pocketed the compass and folded the map, then plunged back into the undergrowth.

The air was warm and wet feeling, like a towel that had been pulled from the dryer before the timer had gone off. It smelled good though: pine needles and the smell of dried leaves underfoot and a faint hint of something floral on the too-infrequent breeze. Mosquitoes had been replaced with flies. These buzzed around her every time she stopped moving. She tried not to very frequently.

If the map was right—or rather, if Emily was reading it correctly—she should be over halfway to the summit of Diablo Point. The sun crept behind the clouds suddenly and left everything around her bleached of color. Emily licked her lips and plodded forward. She tried not to think about

Shawn's last day here. That she might be walking in his exact footsteps—the ones that had carried him to his death —and instead focused on Gracelyn.

What had her daughter been thinking? Emily sighed. If she had a nickel for every time she'd thought that over the years…She shook her head. The answer this time was obvious: revenge. Emily should have known when Gracie had asked Roger to help her brush up on her shooting skills. Emily should have realized then that something was up. But she'd just been so grateful that Gracelyn had stuck around —and especially that she'd wanted to spend time with Roger—that Emily hadn't questioned it. And Roger had been so pleased. Emily remembered the smile on his face when they'd come back in after an especially good practice.

"She can do it with her eyes closed," he'd bragged that night over dinner. "Literally. She closed them and hit the target."

Gracelyn hadn't said much, just smiled benignly and asked Emily to pass the mashed potatoes. Mack had been impressed and Sadie had *oohed* and *ahhed*, telling the twins that someday Daddy would teach them to shoot too, just like Auntie Gracelyn.

The toe of Emily's boot caught and she stumbled. Putting her hands out instinctively, she gripped the rough bark of a tree. It dug into her hands and she pulled them away as soon as she'd gotten her footing. A sharp edge poked out from the side of the big, old tree. Emily frowned and leaned forward again, pulling back some hanging wild grapevines. Underneath she saw a sign, crooked and hand-lettered, so faded it was nearly impossible to read. Emily squinted and ran her fingers over the letters. "G-O" then two letters she couldn't make out. Then, "CK". What in the world…

Gock? Then a cold, sick feeling washed over her. She could just faintly make out the "b" and the "a". "Go back," the sign said. Go back.

She wished she could.

~

JUST OVER TWO HOURS LATER, Emily reached Hidden Lake. She could barely see the steepest part of the mountain overhead. It looked far away—depressingly far—and Emily rolled her shoulders after letting her pack slip from them. Leaving the pack near the overgrown trail that led to the lake, she stretched her arms as she walked. Her back ached. Her feet ached. In fact, there wasn't a part of Emily except maybe her face that didn't.

The "beach" at Hidden Lake was narrow and littered with stone in various sizes. Big rocks stuck out of the ground, perfect for laying on after a frigid dip in the mountain water. She closed her eyes for a moment, reveling in the scent of the slightly fishy-water and the iron-scent coming from the rocks. She'd come here with friends once as a teenager. A dare—to see how far up the mountain they could get. She remembered the noises in the twilight. Then the whispers as they'd packed up and run back down the mountain. Those days seemed like another lifetime—one lived by some other person—most of the time.

Emily crouched, trailed her fingers through the icy water. It dripped from her fingertips, making little circles that ran into one and another over and over again. The woods were quiet here. The ruckus of the birds and the sound of the insects had died away. Here, the air was still, peaceful.

Except...Emily felt the hair on the back of her neck stand

up. She turned. It felt like something was watching her. She scanned the woods behind her and then the sharp cliff that rocketed up hundreds of feet into the higher mountain. Nothing was there. At least, nothing that Emily could see.

She went to retrieve her pack. It was good she'd made it as far as Hidden Lake, where she intended to make camp for the night. She'd get an early start in the morning and should make the summit of Diablo Point just an hour or two after sunrise.

Gracelyn needs you.

The words cut through the air around Emily. She whirled around, expecting to see someone standing by a pine tree or sitting on one of the large stones.

Don't wait, the voice said. Then again, *Gracelyn needs you.*

Emily blinked and looked more closely around her surroundings. She saw something moving in the leaves by a faraway rock, but seconds later a squirrel popped its head out of the leaves and scampered off.

Nothing else moved.

No one stood near her, or even far away for that matter.

So, who had spoken?

Shawn? An angel?

Emily closed her eyes, willing the grittiness to disappear and took a single deep, shaky breath.

Her body was tired and throbbed with every movement. But if that voice—whoever's it was—was right and Gracelyn needed her...how could she stay?

"Whoever you are...if you're real—I'm...I'm going to need some help." She whispered the words into the mild breeze that had picked up. She was half afraid the voice would respond and half afraid it wouldn't.

She waited a few seconds.

Nothing.

Her body still ached. Her feet still felt tired and bruised. But as Emily picked up the heavy pack, she did feel something—a change deep inside her. A calmness. Like a small lamp had been lit and was casting its warm glow throughout her core.

DUSK WAS FALLING as Emily climbed to the last portion of the trail before the steep hike to the summit. Here, the trees and scraggly undergrowth broke with slippery shale that encircled the top of the mountain. The summit itself looked something like the mountain in *How The Grinch Stole Christmas,* pointed, with an exaggerated tilt to it. Emily half expected to find a shaggy, green body perched on the edge, glaring down at her.

Instead, she saw only a steeper incline to climb. Far, far above, a ragged black speck was barely visible in the side of the mountain. Diablo Point tunnel.

Emily swallowed hard and kept climbing.

25

GRACELYN EDWARDS

DIABLO POINT TRAIL

Present Day

Gracelyn opened her eyes. At least, she thought she had. But around her, the world was in total blackness. She blinked once, twice, three times. Nothing had changed. Was she breathing? Her ears were ringing too loudly for her to hear. Where was she?

She tried to move her lips but they were frozen in place. Frantically, she reached her arms out...only to realize she couldn't. She was paralyzed. Completely frozen in place. Blind and paralyzed.

A fly. Gracelyn felt a hysterical laugh bubbling up but even that wouldn't come out. She'd once studied a spider's web in the barn. It was shortly after reading, *Charlotte's Web*, and her nine-year-old mind had been captivated by the intricate, lacey design the barn spider had created. She'd marveled at it daily, seeing it progress from first a couple of strands of stickiness into breathtaking art. But then one morning she'd seen something in the web. Stuck onto the long, delicate fibers a small fly tried to free itself. Instead, it became more and more ensnared. It buzzed—loudly at first and tried to flap its tiny wings—but it was useless. When Gracelyn had gone back later to check on it, to try to free it after chores were done, it had been too late. The little fly was being eaten by the small, black spider.

She willed herself to move something now. A finger. A toe. Anything. She tried to scream. Putting all her energy into it, Gracelyn heard a noise come from her throat.

"Hhh…" and then her breath gave out. "Hhh…" she tried again.

And again.

And again.

Nothing.

Gracelyn wanted to scream. But even that was impossible. Instead, she could do only two things: blink and breathe.

Despite the wall of panic that had descended her heartbeat was slow and regular. Gracelyn thought about that. An effect of the venom. It must slow its prey's pulse. She remembered the raccoon suddenly, in the tunnel. The way the snake had attached it to the earthen wall. How it had stared out from its prison, only its eyes showing any sort of life. She remembered their packs, what was inside of Mack's and wanted to scream again in frustration.

Think. She had to think this through. There must be something…Some way out of this. What did she have to use? Gracelyn had learned this tactic a long time ago when she'd first gotten serious about backpacking. When you got into a pinch, the most important rule was not to panic. Panicking on a trail, in a tight spot could easily get you seriously injured…or worse. The second most important thing: assess what you have and use it. That could mean gear but also anything in your physical environment.

Gracelyn closed her eyes, then opened them again. Though it was minuscule, she could see a variation in the light. That meant that they were in a dark place, not that her vision had stopped working completely. It smelled too, loamy and dank, like old earth. There was another smell too, far stronger: that same stench of dead things. The tunnel then on Diablo Peak. It had to be. Though she couldn't see above or below her, there was a sense of wideness in the walls. They must be deep in though, not near the front or rear where light would pour in.

Unless...

Was it nighttime?

Gracelyn strained to see in the blackness around her. Yes. It was night. Squinting hard, she could barely make out a few faraway stars, their light dull and blurry in her eyes. Either that or it was a mirage based on her longing.

Still, it had to be fairly far from the tunnel's entrance or exit. Otherwise, she'd smell the fresh air. The air here was stale and old. How long would it be before the snake returned? And why hadn't it eaten her already? Unless it intended to save her as a pantry item. Perhaps it was even now feeding the mountain lion to the existing juveniles. Or maybe it had kept that for its own meal. Visions of Mack and the lithe snakes filled her mind but she shoved back against them as hard as she could. Thinking about him...it would end her. And right now she had to focus everything she had on getting the hell out of here.

Suddenly, something scrabbled against her leg. Gracelyn instinctively cried out but of course, no sound came from her throat. Whatever it was, it felt like it was tiptoeing over first her leg and then her ribcage. Then the feeling disappeared. Whatever it was must have—

Wait a second.

She had felt that. Her legs, her side—the venom was wearing off, at least in part. She tried again to move her leg. Yes! Her foot jerked just a little and she felt the motion travel up her calf and into her thigh. Okay. This was good.

But would it be enough? How long until she could walk? She'd go immediately to the back of the tunnel, get Mack's pack and set the charge on the explosives. Gracelyn wasn't entirely sure she knew what to do, but would do it anyway. If there was even a chance she could kill that thing—

A noise from ahead of her, outside the tunnel.

The snake. It was coming back.

Gracelyn moved her legs frantically, straining as hard as she could. Her right leg moved with a feeble jerk and then fell limp again.

No. No. No.

The sound was getting closer. She could see a faint change in the light ahead. The dark gray toward the tunnel's entrance was being blotted out by something even darker.

Rocks and stones clinked together softly. The snake's big body must be sliding into the tunnel.

Gracelyn closed her eyes.

No. No. No.

Not like this. She needed to finish this. She couldn't die here. Not now!

"Gracelyn?" a voice called quietly into the tunnel.

26

EMILY EDWARDS

DIABLO POINT

Present Day

"Gracelyn, are you here?" Emily called softly and picked her way through the stones littering the entrance. A smell wafted from the space: like stale earth and something foul and rotting. She grimaced and poked her head into the tunnel.

The powerful beam of her headlight illuminated the space, washing it almost white. More stones lining the floor of the tunnel, a larger more open space than she'd imagined from the outside. The walls were rough. Roots dangled in a few spots and from these, cobwebs were tangled. She walked further into the tunnel, half-bent at the waist.

Her legs ached and trembled. The farm kept her fit, but it was different than lugging a heavy pack up a mountain peak. The tunnel was narrowing. Already, Emily could feel its walls growing closer and more confining. She hated it. Hated tight, dark spaces. She'd made Roger promise that he'd have her cremated. The thought of spending years inside a box plunked six feet underground made her skin break out in hives.

She slipped her backpack off. Instantly, she felt relief in her back and shoulders. There was a noise, something further ahead. Emily stopped and listened.

Nothing.

She moved again, trying hard to move more quietly over the stones. It was impossible to be soundless given the situation, but she still tried.

What was that? She stopped, listened hard.

"Hhh..."

"Gracelyn?" Emily called out. "Gracelyn, is that you?"

Another moan. Definitely, definitely a moan. Emily pushed forward as fast as the crab walk posture allowed. There! Ahead of her on the tunnel floor, she saw a flash of red and a pair of hiking boots.

"Gracie?"

Emily slid her pack off her back as she drew nearer. Gracelyn lay on her stomach, feet toward Emily. Her hair was tangled with bits of branches and dead leaves. Her face was turned to the tunnel's wall and she moaned again. Emily scooted forward and put a hand on her head. She leaned down, kissing her daughter's exposed cheek and forehead. "Oh baby girl," she said as tears streamed down her face. "Oh, Gracelyn. You scared me to death, do you know that?"

Gingerly, Emily rolled Gracelyn onto her back. She looked fine—no blood, no bones sticking out anywhere they shouldn't be. So what was wrong with her?

"What happened? Is it your head?" A concussion maybe. Gracelyn had had one before, in high school. Emily tried and failed to remember the signs.

Gracelyn's eyes were open but when she tried to form words her mouth opened only a slit.

"Are you hurt?" Emily patted her body down lightly. It was a stupid question. Of course, she was hurt. But where?

"Did you hit your head?"

No response.

Emily ran her fingers lightly over her daughter's head, feeling for cuts or bumps. But there was nothing there. She checked the rest of Gracelyn's body: no marks, no blood. Except...there was a small tear in the fabric on Gracelyn's side. Emily looked more closely, the bright beam illuminating the area. There was a large, red welt there. What in the world...?

Emily sat back, thinking. Gracelyn seemed stunned or in shock. She might have fallen...but how? The tunnel wasn't even tall enough to stand up in. But the mark on her side. It was the only thing Emily had found. What would have caused it, she wondered. Emily bit her bottom lip.

I need help, she thought. I can't get her out of here on my own.

Gracelyn's leg spasmed, jerked violently and then went still.

"Gracie, can you move your legs or arms?"

Gracelyn stared up at Emily but remained motionless.

Okay, that was a no.

"We're getting out of here, I promise. I don't know if this is a mountain lion's tunnel or a bear's but something that likes meat lives here. It's not safe for you and me to stay. Blink once if you understand me."

Gracelyn blinked.

"Okay, that's good. We're not that far from the entrance of the tunnel. I'm going to pull you out that way. I'm not sure what we'll do after that—it's pretty steep—but we'll worry about it then."

Gracelyn blinked once more.

"I'll go as fast as I can, okay? But this probably isn't going to be comfortable."

Emily grasped her daughter's ankles and started to pull. Her lucky red socks were caked with mud that crumbled under Emily's fingers. Her daughter was surprisingly heavy and Emily grunted as she pulled her toward the entrance of the tunnel.

She tried to think of a solution for the steep drop off that awaited them. She couldn't carry Gracelyn down it. She'd had a hard enough time climbing up it. If Emily had a rope maybe she could fashion a sort of pulley. She was so tired she couldn't remember the contents of her pack. Also, the tunnel was giving her serious heebie-jeebies. She expected to see a bear or some other big, scary animal poke its head through the tunnel's entrance at any moment.

Breathing hard, Emily saw her backpack ahead. She tried pushing it to the side and squeeze Gracelyn's body past, but the pack was too big and blocked the way. Instead, Emily let go of Gracelyn's ankles and got the bag, carrying it to the tunnel's entrance. She was about to drop it when a sound filled the air.

It started out softly. Like a gentle whir or swish...almost like the dishwasher made, but much quieter. What was it? Emily peered back past Gracelyn but couldn't see anything. Bats? Emily shivered. Something else she hated about enclosed spaces like caves and tunnels.

The noise grew louder. Something rough sliding against something smooth. Emily thought of her grandmother's work-roughened hands when they slid over a fine satin or silk fabric in her sewing machine. She stared into the tunnel. And then her heart stopped. In the beam of the headlamp maybe ten feet from Gracelyn's head, a set of glittering eyes stared back at her.

It took a few seconds for Emily to understand what she was seeing. She'd expected the eyes to be attached to a furry body. Something darkly colored—a badger or raccoon or worse, a stray coyote or bear. But they weren't. Instead, the eyes shone out of a triangular face set above a long, slender neck. The neck went on and on and on.

No, not a neck then, Emily heard her brain reason it out as though she was a particularly slow child. That was a body. A snake. One bigger than Emily had ever seen before... too large to be real. It was light grayish-green in color and at that moment, it flicked its tongue out of its mouth. It was forked but black rather than pink. As its tongue sampled the air, it revealed a row of very sharp, extremely pointed white teeth. Like sharks' teeth. Two rows of them.

The sight of that jerked Emily into action. She pulled Gracelyn's ankles with all of her strength. Something popped in her low back and started to burn. Emily ignored it and pulled harder.

"Mmm..." Gracelyn moaned.

The snake was getting closer. It writhed and slithered over the stone floor with ease and surprising speed.

"Mmm..."

When Emily was within four feet of the pack, she dropped her daughter's ankles and lunged toward it. Hands scrabbling over the clasps and drawstring, Emily groped and pulled and twisted, until she'd made enough room to shove a hand into the backpack. She pulled the old pistol—her father's—from the bag and aimed it at the snake's head. As though sensing her intentions it dropped low to the ground, its head and body nearly disappearing behind Gracelyn's prone form.

Emily took three shaky steps forward.

"Gracelyn?" Her voice shook. "Gracelyn, there is a really big snake behind you. But I'm going to get you out of here. I'm going—"

Suddenly, the snake shot toward Emily. It was as though it had become a spring and propelled itself up, over Gracelyn and directly towards Emily's face. She screamed, instinctively throwing her arms up over her head. The gun flew from her hands and landed with a thud somewhere nearby. Then something wet and muscular grabbed Emily's ankle. She looked down, horrified to see the tongue of the snake was wound firmly around her ankle. The tongue constricted, jerked her backward. She tripped, lost her balance. She fell awkwardly against the side of the cave. Her hands scrabbled over the floor for the gun. They came away empty.

"No! No!" Emily screamed, her voice bouncing around the tight space. Using her other foot, Emily kicked as hard as she could. Her blow missed the snake's nose where she'd aimed. Instead, it hit it solidly in the left eye. The snake made a horrible sound, part hiss, part scream. Its tongue released her leg. Emily sagged back in momentary relief.

"Mmmom..." Gracelyn moaned.

The snake was writhing on the floor, using its long tongue to try to wipe away the gunk around its eye. Mud? Blood? Emily couldn't tell and didn't spend time figuring it out. Instead, she shone the light around the floor of the tunnel. There! The pistol was just a couple of feet away. She grabbed it and raised it toward the snake. It turned its good eye toward her, the unfathomably long tongue grazing the air near Gracelyn.

"Don't you touch my daughter," Emily muttered. With a shaking breath, she pulled the trigger.

The sound thundered through the tunnel. The force of the explosion nearly knocked Emily backward. It did slam her shoulder into the rough wall. Dirt cascaded down from the ceiling of the tunnel and coated Emily and everything else.

The snake was writhing on the ground, wriggling from one side to the other like a worm on the end of a fish hook. Deafened, Emily shook her head and got into a crouch again. She lined up the pistol's barrel with the snake's trashing body and shot it again. It stopped moving. But Emily didn't. She shot it again and again and again until she, at last, pulled the trigger and there was only a half-muted "click".

Emily lay down on the tunnel floor next to Gracelyn. Every part of Emily's body was shaking. She could feel wetness on her cheeks and between her legs where her bladder had released.

She'd done it. The snake was dead. It had been real—as strange as that sounded—but now it was dead.

"Mom?" Gracelyn's voice was little more than a whisper.

"Yes, baby, I'm right here." Emily put a hand over her daughter's forehead. "It's all over now. The snake is dead."

27

GRACELYN EDWARDS

DIABLO POINT

Present Day

Forty minutes had passed and Gracelyn held her mother's hand. She'd told her about Mack, his showing up and that he'd died, trying to save her. But she couldn't tell her mother everything—it was too fresh and she'd choked when she'd tried. Her words came out in dry, ragged gasps. She wasn't sure why she couldn't cry like a normal person. It seemed that would be cleansing. But maybe it had been too long. Maybe her body had forgotten how.

Now, they rested by two scraggly pine trees in the dark woods. It felt like it had taken them ages to successfully navigate the slippery peak. Emily had used gravity to her advantage, rigging up a sort of stretcher with her pack and some branches, to slide Gracelyn down the steepest parts.

The feeling had started coming back to Gracelyn's limbs. Finally. Now everything felt achy, like when she had the flu.

There was still tingling and numbness in her fingers and toes, but that too, was slowly wearing off.

Emily brushed another kiss—the hundredth?—over Gracelyn's forehead. Gracelyn squeezed her mother's hand in response.

"I'm sorry, Mom," she said. "I might as well have killed Mack myself. And Dad. When I asked him to come here I never thought—"

"Shh," her mother replied and squeezed her hand in response. "It wasn't your fault. None of this is. I'm so very, very sorry about Mack. He was a really special guy and I know you loved him. And he loved you, very much."

Gracelyn felt another dry sob get stuck in her throat. She closed her eyes.

"And I know I've said some really terrible things to you about your father. I'm sorry. I was so angry. Angry that it happened, that he was taken from me—from us—and I needed to blame someone. First I blamed God, but he's not really good at fighting back, so I turned on you."

They sat in silence for a few long minutes. Both lost in their own thoughts. Both Gracelyn suspected, thinking about her father and how much they wished he was here with them now. Somehow thinking about him made it easier to avoid thinking about Mack.

Gracelyn opened her eyes and drew a deep breath. She'd need to wrap her mind around this eventually. Need to come to terms with the fact that he was really gone. But not now. She couldn't allow herself that luxury. And to be honest, she still couldn't quite believe it was real. Any of it.

"I didn't even know you knew how to shoot a gun," Gracelyn said.

Emily laughed abruptly, the sound strange in the stillness of the night.

"I can't really. Your grandfather taught me when I was a kid, but haven't shot a gun in years. Your father took Roger target shooting all the time. He used to ask me to go, but you were little and I didn't want to bother trying to find a sitter. It was easier to just make excuses. But I guess I did okay, huh?"

"Yeah."

They sat in silence for a few more minutes, then Gracelyn spoke again.

"We should get out of here before it comes back."

"Before what comes back, baby?"

Gracelyn paused, swallowed hard. "The snake."

The summer air caressed their skin and wafted away the scent of dirt and decay. Emily sat forward from the trunk of the nearest tree.

"What do you mean? I killed it."

"You killed one. I think it was the largest of the juveniles. But there were two juveniles left—the ones that got Mack—and then there's...the mother."

There was absolute silence for a moment. Gracelyn felt her mother's weight sag against her.

"You mean—"

"The adult is still out there—out here—somewhere."

"But the snake could be anywhere," Emily's voice sounded defeated, tired. "Up in that tunnel, halfway down the mountain. It could have gone back to The Settlement—"

"Wait, what?" Gracelyn interrupted. "What do you mean The Settlement?"

Her mother didn't respond right away. When she did, it was with a heavy sigh.

"Your father said he'd discovered where it had lived once when he was a teenager. He said he'd seen signs of it in one of the old abandoned houses in The Settlement. Another boy had dared him to go into the town with him, walk around. You know how kids are. I hadn't really thought there was a snake back then, so I didn't pay much attention...I never...I never expected this." Gracelyn heard the nylon of her mother's jacket swish and pictured her wiping her eyes.

"What do you remember about what Dad told you?"

Emily sighed again. "Nothing specifically about that day. But there were stories about The Settlement and this mythical snake. The people who've lived in Bondville the longest, they perpetuated the myths, the folklore, until the stories became more real than the people who lived and breathed right next door."

"But it's not all folklore is it, Mom?" Gracelyn's voice was quiet. "Tell me what Dad told you. About the snake and The Settlement. Please."

Emily cleared her throat. "It's probably best to start at the beginning." She stayed quiet for a few long minutes.

"Bondville is old but The Settlement is even older. People—your father's ancestors among them—came to Bondville to escape the bedlam at Salem. And into the mix was added misfits—people who'd lived on the fringes of society and settled themselves here, near the mountains. There were clashes at first, but eventually, both sides came to see it would be smarter to stick together out here than to live in constant conflict. So they learned to live together in Bondville, in peace most of the time.

"The people in The Settlement were different though. They kept to themselves, but in an entirely different way. They created their own language. They'd cut off all contact with the outside world. And..." Emily's voice faded. "And," she continued. "They'd come to depend on a dark magic, a...a spiritualism, to survive."

"What, like witchcraft?" Gracelyn asked.

Emily made an affirmative noise. "I don't think anyone outside the town really knows what it was: witchcraft, voodoo, druidism, or something else entirely. But it was scary stuff. At first, the most resolute of the Puritans had tried to make contact. To share their faith with the people of The Settlement but you can imagine how well that went over.

"Tensions continued to rise. Despite the desire for peace, the townspeople in Bondville were afraid of their neighbors. You have to remember, they'd just escaped a community torn apart by witchcraft. They were overly sensitive maybe to their neighbors' choices.

"Eventually there was talk of going to burn down The Settlement, drive out the evil spirits and save the people's souls...or at least get them far away from their homes and families. But something horrible happened that changed their minds."

"What?" Gracelyn asked.

Her mother took a deep breath. "All the children in Bondville died. In one night."

"They killed all their kids?" Gracelyn asked. She heard the sound of nylon on nylon. Her mother was either nodding or shaking her head.

"I can't see you, Mom."

"Sorry, baby," her mother answered. "Yes, they all died. That's the story anyway."

"And so the Bondville townspeople assumed that The Settlement people had done it, using their dark magic," Gracelyn said.

"Yes."

"Had they?"

"I don't know. Maybe. Or it could have been a plague or

outbreak of scarlet fever. Records from that time period aren't in existence so everything I'm telling you is just hearsay."

"Dad would call it 'oral tradition,'" Gracelyn said with a sad smile.

They were quiet a few seconds. A breeze rustled the leaves overhead.

"So, how does all that tie in with the snake?" Gracelyn asked.

"Supposedly the snake was...well, conjured by the people in The Settlement. They cast a deep spell on a real snake or that they sort of, created one of their own. The story goes that they thought..." her voice faded into a chuckle. Gracelyn saw the outline of her mother, rubbing her face with her hands. "The people in Bondville thought that the people in The Settlement had created the snake to steal their children's souls. That it had slithered through their little village and killed them, to send a message to the residents there."

"Stay away?" Gracelyn asked.

"Yes," her mother said. "Or maybe they hoped that their giant serpent would frighten the people of Bondville away, make them run back to wherever they'd come from."

"Why didn't you ever tell me this?" Gracelyn asked.

"Because I didn't believe it myself. A giant snake? Come on. Dark magic in the wilds of Vermont? It's a little far-fetched. You know how it is here anyway. The stories that managed to survive are likely twisted from their original version anyway.

"And your father... Well. It was an area that we never agreed on. I didn't encourage his telling the stories."

Gracelyn wanted to scream in frustration and cry in sadness all at the same time. No wonder her father had been terrified of snakes. No wonder he'd been reluctant to climb Diablo Point with her. She'd heard whispers of the stories growing up. But it was more schoolyard spookiness and campfire tales.

Strangely enough, it was only after leaving Vermont after high school that Gracelyn had learned of the supposed giant snake that lived in the mountain. If she'd realized all this back then, would she still have gone looking for it? Yes, probably. Knowing about the past—about the legends— wasn't the same as experiencing it for yourself. And she would have never truly believed the tale of the snake was real if she hadn't had this encounter.

28

GRACELYN EDWARDS

DIABLO POINT

Present Day

Gracelyn's head pounded. She was dehydrated and the water bottle in her pack stuck in the tunnel wasn't going to help. She rubbed a hand over her forehead which felt gritty from dirt and dried sweat.

"We need to make a plan. It will be daylight before long and we need water, shelter if we're going to stay—"

"Stay?" Emily's voice interrupted. "What are you talking about? We need to get out of here, get back home. Now, Gracelyn. And no, it's not up for debate."

Gracelyn felt her shoulders stiffen instinctively. How was it that you could go from a full-grown, capable woman back to a child in the space of a few seconds when your parent used a certain tone of voice?

"You should go," Gracelyn said, trying to keep her voice calm and rational. "Roger and Sadie and the girls—they need you. But I'm staying. I came here to kill that snake and I will if it's the last thing I do."

"It may very well be," Emily's voice was tight with anger. She stopped, took a deep breath. When she spoke again her voice was filled with sadness. "I've already lost your dad. You've lost Mack. Please, Gracie, I can't lose you, too."

"You won't, Mom. If we're smart and work together, we can make a plan and kill that thing. Once and for all. Stop it from ever hurting anyone else."

"How?"

"I...I don't know yet. I'm still thinking it through. Mack had explosives in his pack—"

Gracelyn felt her mother's body stiffen beside her. "What?"

"Just a few." As though that changed things.

"I'm not even going to ask how he got those," Mom said, voice tired.

"It's a long story," Gracelyn said. "But we need to think this through. We're not sure where the snake is at the moment, but I'd guess the second tunnel. Maybe tending to the juvenile it has left."

"The question is, why aren't they out here, looking for us?" her mother said. She waited for a beat, then said, "There is one other possibility. Maybe they live in The Settlement, at least part of the time. No one ever goes to visit the rotting collection of houses left there."

"Good idea. We'll look there, too. But later. We should check these tunnels first. And I need to get to the backpacks."

"So, how are we planning to divert the snakes' attention while tossing explosives at it? Oh, and get ourselves out of the tunnel before the whole thing collapses on us?"

Gracelyn hid her smile, even though it was dark. The

fact her mother was using terms like, "we" and "our" meant she was on board. Still, she had a point. The element of surprise was the best thing they'd had going for them…and that was long gone.

"We'll figure it out as we go," Gracelyn said, knowing how weak that sounded. You didn't just "figure it out as you go" when you were in a life or death situation like this. But what other choice did they have? Every minute they sat here guessing and second-guessing and not moving was giving the snake a better chance at getting away. Or getting them.

As if on cue, a sound broke the stillness of the night. It was a now-familiar sound: something large and heavy sliding over the ground. It whispered through the leaves. Rocks clinked together. Gracelyn's heart skipped a beat and then thundered on.

"It's coming." Gracelyn had barely whispered when she heard snatches of words: "father" and "protect us". It was Mom, she realized, whispering a prayer over and over like a mantra.

"Move!" Gracelyn grabbed at the air near where Emily had been seated, but her hands came away empty.

"Go," her mother said, her voice firm, her tone without waver. "Find the packs, get the explosives. I'll lead it away from you. Yell to me when you're ready and I'll run in that direction."

"No, Mom, I—"

"Now, Gracie," Mom said.

"The rear of the main tunnel! That's where I'm going. I'll go out the front and set up the charge there." Gracelyn took one stumbling step forward, then another. The headlamp she'd put on was clear and powerful but everything around her was still dim and cast in shadows. She heard her mother moving off to the west of them, toward the smaller tunnel.

She yelled gibberish and clapped her hands, trying to draw the snake's attention.

Would this work? Gracelyn felt a deep urge to pull away and run back toward her mother, toward the snake that was hunting her. Wanted to plunge a sharp stick into its eye or drive a bullet into its skull.

She couldn't do any of those things though, not now. So she scrabbled up the mountain and prayed to a God she didn't even believe in to save them all. To please, please save her mother even if Gracelyn didn't make it out alive.

Though she was moving as fast as possible, the tunnel's exit seemed an impossibly long way away. She could still smell the leftover scent of gunpowder in the air. The sun was just beginning to turn the sky to the east a soft shade of pearl gray tinged with pink when she finally arrived, breathless, at the tunnel's exit. She didn't wait but plunged into the dark tube. The light bounced along the tunnel walls. She counted her steps as she crab-jogged through the space. Tried not to imagine that the tunnel itself was a huge snake and that she'd just walked directly into its throat.

Finally, too many long minutes later, she reached the packs. She couldn't carry both, so left hers and took Mack's. She shoved it along the floor ahead of her when the tunnel grew even more narrow. She expected to see a set of glittering eyes—the juvenile snake was still out there somewhere—around every corner. But the tunnel was empty as far as she could tell.

As Gracelyn crawled, she planned: she'd leave the pack with the explosives charged and ready to detonate outside the entrance of the cave. Hopefully, their scent on the bag and gear would draw the snake. She'd need to do something to draw it though—maybe yell and scream, maybe cut her arm or leg. Was it drawn to blood like a shark, she wondered. The word "shark" made a picture of the snake's sharp rows of teeth appear. She skidded, lost her footing and tripped down the rest of the tunnel to the entrance. Where was Mom? Was she okay? Gracelyn hadn't heard anything—a cry for help, a scream—and hoped that meant she was all right.

Gracelyn herself had made good time, better than before. Adrenaline pushed her faster but it also made it easier for mistakes to happen. She forced herself to walk through the steps of the plan: step one: arm the explosives. Step two: attract the attention of the snake. Step three—

A cry cut through the early gray morning. Gracelyn felt as though ice water had been dumped over her. She stopped, listened.

"Mom?"

Another cry split the air.

"Mom!" Gracelyn cried out. She lunged forward, slid and slipped down the shale underfoot. She ran as fast as her legs would move toward the sound of her mother's cries. The terrain under her feet switched suddenly from stones to earth. Gracelyn picked up her pace, pumped her arms, scanned the forest in front of her. She looked for any sign of her mother. Or the snake.

Suddenly, the earth beneath Gracelyn opened.

She'd stumbled.

Then she screamed.

Her body fell and was swallowed by a hole in the earth.

29

EMILY EDWARDS
DIABLO POINT

Present Day

Emily wiped a hand over her mouth which was sour from vomit. She turned away from the tunnel's entrance and spit. Her throat felt raw from both the screaming and getting sick.

She'd run this way, thinking she could find refuge—or at least a temporary weapon—closer to the tunnel Gracelyn had told her about. Instead, she'd found the remains of Mack and a second dead snake, this one blown to bits. Her mind hadn't registered it at first. She'd stared at the carnage, her brain whirling. Then she'd realized. Gracelyn had just told her that he'd died, but she'd been too broken up to tell her how and Emily hadn't asked.

She looked over her shoulder, sure she'd see a massive serpentine body following her. But the woods were quiet and still.

Where had it gone? What if she'd guessed wrong and the snake had followed Gracie instead of Emily?

She scanned the woods slowly, looking for anything moving, any tree branches or undergrowth shaking.

There!

The leaves on a bunch of birch trees shivered, then another bunch further up and to the right did the same. The snake must be there, in the undergrowth. Emily followed behind, giving it a wide berth. She stepped carefully and with care, trying not to give herself away. Using the tree trunks, Emily pulled herself upward. The incline grew steeper here. If Gracelyn had—

There she was! Gracie was coming down the mountain, headed in Emily's direction. She was moving quickly over the stones, but quietly, more quietly than Emily could have imagined possible. Emily waved her arms but didn't make any noise.

Look this way. Look over here, Gracie!

Leaves and branches on the undergrowth shook. Emily started to call out, to warn Gracelyn—

Gracelyn cried out.

And then she disappeared.

Emily frantically searched the area where her daughter had been standing. Where had she gone? She hurried forward, not bothering to be as quiet now.

Then, a horrible thought: had the snake gotten her?

No, it was still too far away. Even now, Emily could see the branches and leaves still moving, still yards away from where she'd last seen Gracelyn.

~

EMILY'S back was so sore, she wasn't sure she'd ever stand up straight again. She'd been searching the woods for long minutes, looking for any signs—footprints, a fragment of fabric, a bent branch—anything that would tell her where Gracelyn had gone.

She couldn't have just disappeared into thin air. And yet, that's what this felt like. Emily had found the pack at the entrance of another tunnel, the big one on Diablo Peak. But there was no sign of her daughter anywhere. There was no sign of the snake either.

It was only a short distance from the second mountain when Emily saw it. At first, she thought her eyes were playing tricks on her. An opening in the ground, half-covered in leaves and tree debris. It was large, like a manhole, the edges soft and worn down. As though something used it frequently and had smoothed away the rough sides.

"Oh, no." Emily rushed to the side of it, dropped to her stomach and peered in. The tunnel dropped straight down but then became too dark to see further. Impossible as it was to believe, it looked like a mine shaft. But why? Why would there be a mine shaft here in the middle of nowhere? Had the old settlers used the lake as a quarry? But even so, they wouldn't have used a tunnel-like this...Emily tried to remember all she could about early mining but came up empty. Whatever it was and whoever had made it, she was pretty sure that Gracelyn had fallen into it. She looked around the area carefully. There! A little piece of red lint, from Gracelyn's socks, had snagged on a low-hanging branch near the hole.

Emily unstrapped her pack and found a length of rope.

Tying one end around a tree, she swallowed hard and tested her weight. The rope creaked but held. She slowly lowered herself down into the tunnel. When the rope had only two feet left of give, Emily planted her knees and arms against the tunnel walls. Every part of her shook with exertion. The smell of the earth so close to her, the feeling of things scuttling over her exposed skin...she wasn't going to make it. She swallowed a scream and used all her strength to climb upward. She pictured the rope above fraying, her body tumbling down, down, down into the abyss below. Or if not the rope, then the snake. Appearing above her, blocking out the sunlight, its forked tongue sampling the air that carried her smell...

When she'd finally hauled herself back onto the leaf-strewn ground, Emily, half-crying, half-laughing in relief, rolled over on her back. She had to come up with a new plan. It was a gamble, but it had to be better than falling down the rest of that tunnel.

If she was right, Emily would find Gracelyn. If she was wrong...

Well. She wasn't going to think about that.

30

EMILY EDWARDS

DIABLO POINT TRAIL

Present Day

S he hurried downhill before she changed her mind. A little voice in her head told her to stop, slow down, to think this through. But her instincts told her to go. Legs shaking, sweat dripping into her eyes, Emily half jogged, half bushwhacked down the mountainside. She kept her pace as steady as possible, even though her body wanted her to stop and her heart wanted her to sprint.

Emily remembered suddenly the stupid dare she'd accepted shortly after moving to Bondville. One of the other girls, Chanice Baker, had taken an instant disliking to Emily. Chanice had been the most popular girl in their class.

"I'll bet you can't walk through The Settlement by yourself," Chanice had said, as the small group walked home after school.

Emily had just smiled.

"At night," Chanice added.

Coldness had crept over Emily's skin but she tried not to let her fear show. Bullies loved to know they had the upper hand. Besides, Emily didn't believe any of the ghost stories about The Settlement. Why would it bother her to walk through the place?

Just because it was deserted.

And supposedly haunted by the spirits of the people who used to live there.

And possibly a giant, man-eating snake.

Emily had forced her smile to remain in place. "Sure," she'd said, hoping Chanice and the others couldn't hear her thundering heartbeat. "When?"

"How about this Friday?" Chanice had asked, her lips curled up into a cat-like smile. "It's the thirteenth."

"Really? I bet there's a full moon expected, too."

"Nah," Chanice had blown her teased bangs out of her eyes. "But it might rain, so you'd better bring your umbrella."

Emily had joked and laughed with the other kids in the group for the next hour outside of the little general store that also served as a post office. But when she was walking home alone, Shawn had caught up to her.

"Hey," he'd said, glancing at her and then away, his cheeks pink.

"Hi."

"You know you don't have to do it if you don't want to."

Emily knew exactly what he was talking about but pretended not to.

"Do what?"

"The solo walk in The Settlement. I mean, I can go with you. If you want. Or you could tell Chanice that you'll only do it if one of your friends goes with you. Like Lizette or Barb—"

"No thanks."

They walked in silence a few steps. "Aren't you scared?" Shawn asked. "I mean, to go in by yourself?"

Emily had shaken her head. "Not really. But thanks. Thanks for offering to go with me. I'll be fine." Scared didn't begin to cover it, but Emily wasn't about to tell anyone that. Besides, Shawn had done it himself, the second day after she'd started school here. And he'd lived to tell the tale.

"Okay," Shawn had said and Emily wondered if she'd imagined the disappointment in his voice.

He was cute in a farm-kid kind of way. She knew his parents owned the big farm further down the road from where her family was. They'd lived in the area for generations her mother had told Emily's dad. Mom had been overwhelmed since they moved in and had asked for Shawn's mother's advice more than once.

Emily had turned and smiled at Shawn. "Thanks again for offering. It was sweet."

His cheeks had turned dark red and he'd stumbled, catching the toe of his sneaker on a stone in the road.

"No problem," he'd said. Then, "Let me know if you change your mind."

But Emily hadn't.

She'd walked down the lonely, dark streets of The Settlement that Friday night while her friends huddled in a little group in a thatch of trees nearby. Emily had swung her flashlight confidently and prowled around the buildings, testing doors to see which were open, then slipping inside those that swung inward. Once indoors, she'd pressed herself against the closest wall, counted to thirty and re-emerged hearing the hoots of encouragement from Shawn and the others.

She'd emerged from the ramshackle gathering of deserted buildings a half-hour later, her cobwebbed head held high. No sign of a snake or a ghost either. She'd walked right up to Chanice and given her a halfhearted hug whispering in the other girl's ear, "Your turn."

Chanice had refused to go in, made excuses about curfew. The others had cast sidelong glances, before surrounding Emily, eventually leaving Chanice behind. Emily had embellished the facts the way any good storyteller would.

Eventually, it was just Emily left, and Shawn, to walk down the dirt road toward their farms. He'd asked if he could hold her hand once they were alone. His palm had been damp in hers but when they got to her mailbox, she'd stepped toward him and planted a dry kiss on his cheek before running lightly to the side shed. Then she'd scaled its roof and climbed back into her open bedroom window like she would many more times in the future.

It all felt like a lifetime ago. How had she gone from such a brave, rebellious girl to a grown woman too comfortable in her life to ever experience adventure? Maybe she and Gracelyn were more alike than she'd thought. Or at least, the girl Emily used to be. She'd slowed over the years, become more and more dependent on routine and predictable answers than on the unknown. Maybe Roger had learned that from her, or she'd fed off of his love of stability and laidback attitude. Whatever the reason, Emily wasn't sure if she disliked the fact that she'd changed. She did wonder why. Maybe Bondville had something to do with it. It seemed to get under people's skin, tether them in place.

It was like living in a pit of quicksand, only sinking so slowly that you didn't even realize it was happening.

Emily shook her head. The air around her was slightly cooler and birds were once again singing. She must be getting closer to the start of the trail. And closer, she hoped, to her daughter.

31

EMILY EDWARDS

THE SETTLEMENT

Present Day

E mily repeated the words over and over in her head as she walked through The Settlement: "Though I walk through the valley and the shadow of death, I will fear no evil." That's what the town felt like: the valley and shadow of death. As though the darkness from the past were pushing itself on the town now. She'd made a makeshift spear from a straight, hard branch on her way down the mountain. Emily used it now as a walking stick, keeping the sharp tip pointed upward so it wouldn't get dulled.

The Settlement was decrepit, barely more than rubble in most places. The few structures that still stood leaned precariously or looked ready to cave in completely. Most had already given up the fight, lying in piles of wood and stone as though they'd imploded.

She couldn't remember which building Shawn had said

he'd seen the giant hole. Or maybe he'd never told her specifically which it was. If he'd told her back then before she'd taken up Chanice's dare, would she still have gone in? Yes, probably. Emily wished Shawn were here with her now, that she could ask him.

Light was dawning in the sky, turning the eastern sky a rosy pinkish gray. The streets—or what had been streets— were just choked paths of weeds and saplings now. Only the sound of the stone underfoot and the basic layout of the town helped her identify them.

She'd left Diablo Point trail and crossed through a patch of woods and then down a little further into The Settlement. It looked so different than when she'd last been here as a teenager. She could count only five roof peaks left from where she stood, not far from where she and her friends had been standing all those years ago.

It was hard going through the brush and undergrowth. Vines and thorn bushes grabbed at her pant legs and more than once she stopped to shimmy her way out of their grasp. The air was sweet here. White flowers on different kinds of vines climbed over structures and saplings and scented the air.

Emily ignored the two birds bickering in a tree overhead and made her way to the first house. The houses were tiny compared to modern-day houses and looked like small hunting shacks or summer camps. They were made of logs, but most of the chinking between the beams was missing.

The first house that Emily came to was half sliding into the ground beneath it. A large tree, one that must have once offered lovely shade, had come out of the ground roots and all. It had smashed the rear of the house. Emily hesitated for a second before she pushed through the front door. It squeaked and creaked on its hinges. The sound sent a jolt up Emily's spine.

"Gracelyn?" she called into the empty space. The interior smelled faintly of animal droppings and small rodents. It was dark inside, with just two small windows set far up on the left side. They were covered in a dark film of dirt and bugs and who knew what else. Emily could make out the shadowy shapes of simple furniture: a half-collapsed bed in the far corner, a shelf covered so thickly in cobwebs she couldn't make out what was on it, and closer to the door, a tiny kitchen table with a broken leg. Two chairs lay like lumps in the dirt and grime. Some kind of insect had bored holes all over the wood.

"Gracie?" she called out again. The house, muted in thick dust and grime, absorbed the sound. Emily walked around the room slowly, looking for any signs of tracks or footprints.

She saw nothing.

Leaving the house, she took in big breaths of fresh, pure air. Pushing through the undergrowth to the next building, Emily wished for a machete, or at least a large kitchen knife. The branches and vines moved in a heavy breeze and Emily stiffened, glanced at the sky. The pretty pink sunrise was now smeared with dark clouds. "Red sky in the morning, sailors take warning," Emily said aloud and shivered.

Which one? She looked at the remaining buildings. Which one might have a tunnel in it that led up the mountain? A horrible thought occurred to Emily: could the snake have more babies down here? Another nest? She shoved the thought away and plunged through the thick vegetation to the next house. The door was stuck and it took her several long minutes to push her way through. When she finally did, she was met with a scent: like rotten food and something musky and wild. Emily knew before she saw the door to the cellar below that she'd found the right house. Because all along the floor which was covered with a thick layer of dust and grime were wide tracks.

Tracks made by something very large. Something that had slithered over its surface.

Like the other house, this one was in shambles. Signs of the family who'd once lived here remained though: a broken table, two sagging beds whose straw had been mostly eaten, a pair of moth-eaten curtains even, still hanging from a molded curtain rod.

Emily gripped the makeshift spear and advanced toward the basement door. It was small by modern standards. She'd read about old houses that the pioneers built: some had dug out little root cellars directly under the homes after they were built. They'd stored their foodstuffs underground, to keep them through another winter. This door was tightly closed. But through the middle of it stood a huge, gaping hole. Emily swallowed and flicked on her flashlight. Her hand shook and the beam wobbled.

"Gracelyn?" she called out. Then again, "Gracie?"

She heard nothing at first. But then as though far away, a small cry—of pain? alarm?—and Emily rushed toward the door. She had to put the spear down to grip the old metal handle with two hands. She pulled. Nothing happened. Straining, she did it again and again. Still nothing. It wasn't until Emily shone the light around the edges of the door that she could see why. The door had a bunch of rusted locks, perfectly lined up in a neat row, the nails for each buried deep into the wooden frame.

Emily swallowed and looked from at the hole in the middle of the door. If she was going to get through it, she'd have to crawl. A shiver ran through her just thinking about it. She did not want to do this. Another cry from the other side of the door though, sent her plunging through. There was just enough room for Emily if she twisted her body from right to left, right to left, over and over again. She went in feet first. There was nothing but air under her feet. She shone her flashlight beneath her. A narrow, primitive ladder was secured to the wall beneath the door.

The air here smelled worse than in the house. The basement was pitch black. Something sticky touched Emily's face and she nearly yelped but bit her tongue. Again, faintly, she heard a sound like a sob. *I'm coming, Gracelyn, I'm coming.* She couldn't hold both the flashlight and the spear but wasn't willing to leave either behind. Instead, her right hand gripped the spear. She'd wedged the flashlight between her shirt and jacket collar, using the elastic pull to keep it in place.

The beam of light wobbled over the space in front of her. Emily paused, trying to get her bearings. The space was compact, the walls cut from the ground. She turned her torso slightly to the right and then the left, shining the beam of light into the room.

It was a small room, perhaps twelve by twelve feet, but surprisingly deep. The pebbly bottom of the room was at least twenty feet below her. She stopped and listened but couldn't hear any other sounds. There was a faint noise in the air, like waves of water hitting the shore. What was it?

Quickly, Emily positioned herself to climb down the ladder. The problem was that when she faced it, she couldn't see a thing behind her. But going down backward while clutching the spear wasn't going to work. She'd just have to be fast.

Something hairy brushed her cheek. Emily jerked her head back. A root poked out of the ground above her and she sighed in relief. Below her, the noise like waves grew louder. As she climbed lower, she could make out the sound.

It was hissing. Many things hissing. The sound undulated in waves. Emily clung to the ladder with one hand, using the other to shine the flashlight around the floor of the cellar. It was covered in snakes. They writhed and swiveled in the beam of light. And in the corner of the room, crouching on a large, flat stone counter was Gracelyn.

"Gracelyn?" Emily whispered loudly. Because somewhere in the space or close by had to be the mother snake. "Gracie?"

No response. Then Gracelyn looked toward Emily, her face smeared with dirt. A cut above her left eyebrow dripped rivulets of blood down her cheek.

"Mom?" her voice asked quavering. "Mom, you...you found me."

A mixture of fear and relief filled Emily. "I'm going to get you out of here. Can you—"

"Don't, Mom. Don't come down here. She's coming back —she's close."

"I'm getting you out of here, Gracelyn," Emily repeated. "Can you walk?"

Gracelyn shook her head, then leaned it back against the dirt wall. Her head lolled there and she looked at her mother with half-opened eyes. "It did something to me— the venom again. I can only move from the waist up. And I feel—weird—groggy. Mom, please just go. Get help—"

"No. I'll be damned if I'm going to let that snake get you too."

Emily surveyed the floor beneath her. She didn't know much about snakes, other than the small garters that lived around the farm. They were harmless and ate pests and she and Roger never bothered them. But these...these were different. The light seemed to bother them. They twisted and shrunk back in its beam. They were all different lengths and thicknesses, most brown, some gray and others very dark. A few had stripes but most were dull and unre- markable.

Milk snakes—those were dark brown like some of these —but Emily didn't think these were milk snakes. Were there poisonous snakes here, other than the giant ones? Emily didn't think so. But then, she'd never thought there was such a thing as huge, mammal-eating snakes either. She shivered, took another two steps down. She was about three feet from the bottom of the cellar. She could easily jump down. But didn't want to.

Maybe there was another way to get to Gracelyn. Emily shone the beam around the floor of the cellar again. A few leaning shelves were coming away from the wall on the far side of the space. There were jars, many of which had smashed open, in the process of sliding off of these. An old ladder was propped against another wall and there were wooden boxes and moldering baskets in a pile near that.

The snakes writhed and undulated over each other. Their eyes were strange—whitish. Maybe they were blind. If they'd lived all their lives down here in the earth then this made sense. Still, it seemed like their whole bodies shrank away from the light.

"There are snakes all over the floor," Emily told Gracelyn who nodded.

"I know. I pulled myself up here."

Emily couldn't help but smile. "Good girl. I'm coming toward you now. Just stay put."

"Mom, don't."

But Emily was already moving. Like a Band-Aid, she was

going to do it fast—run to the stone and haul herself up onto it. And then...

"Then what, Mom?" Gracelyn asked as though reading her thoughts. "You can't carry me out of here." They were both quiet a moment. The snakes underfoot hissing and sliding. "How did you get down here? Are there stairs?"

Emily shook her head, then remembered that Gracelyn couldn't see her. "No, a ladder. We're in the basement of one of the houses in The Settlement."

"I figured that part out," Gracelyn said. "I tried to keep track of what direction we were moving when it—when it took me."

Emily counted to three and held her breath. Then, like she was plunging into a freezing river, she lunged toward the safety of the big stone slab. The feeling underfoot was disgusting. Snakes twisted and flopped underfoot. It felt as though Emily were walking on a sheet of muscles. A smaller one was squished under one boot. Another muscled body slapped against her other calf. They twisted around her ankles like thick seaweed. She didn't look down. A tiny snake dropped from the side of the wall above her and fell down around her neck. She flung it off, nearly losing her spear in the process.

Finally, she made it to the stone slab and clambered upward. Gracelyn caught one of her elbows and pulled weakly at it.

"You shouldn't have done that," Gracelyn said as Emily scrabbled onto the stone slab.

Emily's breath was coming hard in her chest, her pulse throbbing wildly in her wrists. "You're right," she half-laughed, half-sobbed. "That was one of the worst experiences of my life."

She put down the flashlight and spear, making sure they

were secure on the stone before she cradled Gracelyn's cheeks in her hands.

"Are you all right?"

Gracelyn nodded. Emily dug in her jacket pocket and found a bandana, then pressed it against the cut on Gracelyn's forehead. "Keep pressure here, okay?"

Gracelyn held weakly onto the bandana and Emily saw the tear tracks on her daughter's face.

"We're going to get out of here," she told her daughter. "We just have to wait for the venom to wear off enough for you to walk. I'm going to stay right here with you. You don't have to worry."

Gracelyn made a choking sound and turned away from her mother. Emily surveyed the room, shining her flashlight over the other walls and giving Gracelyn a chance to collect herself. Crying was a sign of weakness in Gracelyn's opinion. Over the years, Emily had learned to give her daughter space with her emotions.

She studied the area again. Nearest to their place on the stone counter, Emily saw a metal box. Too small to be a trunk, but slightly larger than a modern-day shoebox. It was dull but when the light passed over it the surface glinted. Strange.

If it was metal it was thoroughly corroded now, from the dampness of the room. Emily leaned down. She could just get her fingertips around it.

"They keep going to that," Gracelyn said, her voice low.

"What?"

"The snakes. They keep sliding over it and then going back across the room. It's like they like the feeling of the box or something."

Emily watched.

Gracelyn was right. Like they were taking turns, the

snakes slid one after another across the floor of the base-ment and glided over the metal box. Where their bodies pressed against it, the metal was shinier, less faded.

"Strange," Emily said. Then, "Why don't they climb up here? Surely they could if they wanted."

Gracelyn sniffed once more and used the square of cloth to wipe her face. "I'm not sure," she said. "Maybe the stone is too smooth?"

"Maybe."

Emily reached down again toward the box.

"What are you doing?"

"I don't know," Emily said and pulled on the edge of it. It easily came off the ground and she lifted it onto the stone slab.

"I wonder what's in it?" She tugged at the cover, expecting it to be rusted shut. But it easily opened in her hands. Inside, lay a small, brown book. There were also bunches of dried herbs that crumbled under her fingers, a few mostly burned-down candles and a half-empty bottle of some liquid in a brown jar. The cork was still in place, though it was as hard as stone.

"This is strange," Emily said. She glanced at Gracelyn who was staring unseeingly at the things Emily showed her. "I wonder whose things these were?"

She pulled the brown book free and held it up in the light. Opening the front cover she read, "The Journal of Jerome Lancaster," in a swirly, old-fashioned script.

"Wow, this is—"

"Mom," Gracelyn interrupted, ignoring the pile of detritus in the box. "I just wanted to tell you that if anything happens to me and I—"

"No, don't," Emily said. She tucked the little journal into

her jacket pocket. "Don't talk like that. We're going to get out of here. Can you move your—"

A sound filled the space. Both women jerked. A thick, heavy body moved through the earth. Where was it coming from? It was too close to be in the house above them. But the rest of the four walls of this cellar were solid. Weren't they? So where—

Emily had the answer before she'd finished thinking the rest of the question. Her light beam caught motion on the far wall. She stared in horror. There was a large hole, about three feet up on the wall over the trunk. She hadn't noticed it before because the dirt blended in with the walls made of earth.

Through the hole, two eyes glowed in the light.

32

EMILY EDWARDS

THE SETTLEMENT

Present Day

The huge snake hesitated in the hole, then flicked its long, forked tongue in their direction. Unlike the snakes covering the floor of the basement, this one's eyes were clear, sparkling in the beam of light. Emily wanted to turn it off, cover her ears and rock like she had as a child woken from a nightmare.

"It's here," she whispered instead to Gracelyn. "In a hole on the far wall. About three feet off the floor."

"That must be where we came in," Gracelyn whispered.

Emily's heart throbbed hard in her head. She tried to slow her breathing. She needed to think clearly. Needed to remain calm.

Again the black, forked tongue tested the air.

"Can you move your feet?" Emily asked.

Gracelyn's left foot jerked slightly before returning its

position. "Not really. Mom, please, please leave. You can make it out of here. Chances are it won't go after you—I can make noise, a distraction—you—"

"No."

"But—"

"No way."

The snake moved forward, a graceful glide for such a big body. Emily stared, fascinated as the beast slid through the opening. It was like watching a train: the length of it kept coming and coming until Emily started to feel slightly dizzy.

Then finally, its tail dropped through the hole and into the cellar with the rest of the massive body. Emily kept the flashlight beam on its head—such a huge head—and tried not to let her hand shake. It was an impossible task. Trembling, her hand made the beam of light bounce and sway over the snake and the small sea of them on the floor.

If she'd thought the juvenile snake up in the tunnel was large, this was a T-rex in comparison. It looked around, as though checking the corners of the room to make sure there was no one hiding there. That's what she should have done. Emily cursed herself. She could have laid in wait, hidden herself there until the big snake appeared. Then surprised it.

But just the thought of the wait—with the smaller snakes slithering over her, up her pant legs, twisting themselves over her arms and up her back—made Emily nearly gag.

"What should we do?" Gracelyn asked. Emily couldn't remember the last time Gracelyn had sounded unsure. Or afraid.

"I don't know."

The snake swiveled toward them. Its tongue flicked out,

testing the air inches from Emily's face. She shrank back. She couldn't breathe. Her body felt rigid and stiff like a corpse's.

"Oh God! Help!" Her cry was muted in the earthen space, her words seeming to fall flat. The snake slithered back, then forward, readjusting itself on the floor, lining itself up—to strike? To strangle?—Emily didn't want to find out. She moved forward slightly. Blocked Gracelyn as best she could with her body.

Then she pressed the flashlight into Gracelyn's hand. "Don't move."

Gracelyn's hand was surprisingly steady, the beam of light still on the massive form in front of them.

Emily put both hands on her spear. She wedged the end of it into the wall behind them. The tip pointed out—deadly sharp she hoped—and they waited. The snake watched all of this with interest.

Then it made a sound. It started out low, like a hum. But soon the noise grew louder. The walls of the cellar began to jitter slightly. Small bits of dirt cascaded down.

"What's happening?" Gracelyn cried. "Is it an earthquake?"

"I don't know," Emily said. The snake was frozen in place, its mouth closed, its eyes staring. At first, Emily thought it was staring at them. Then she realized its gaze was slightly to the left, staring at the remains in the little metal box.

The sound made the smaller snakes on the floor go wild. They wove and slithered and bobbed over each other like a madcap sea. Waves of them rolled and ricocheted. As though they were feeding off the energy, the sound in the small space.

The sound went on. A sort of dull, monotone hum like electricity wires, buzzing and vibrating. It was coming from the snake. It rolled toward them like a spool of thread. The sound blocked out other thoughts, made it hard to think about anything but the dull, flat hum. Wait, Emily thought, wait, I needed to do something. She squinted, tried to think through the noise. Then a verse she'd read two days ago came to her. She could see the words, as though they were written on a blackboard across her brain: "But the Lord is faithful, and He will strengthen you and protect you from the evil one."

He will protect us from the evil one. He will protect—

Suddenly, the snake started to move forward. It was as though the strange, loud hum were propelling it. As it jerked toward them, Emily gripped the spear with both hands. A warm, yellow feeling of peace spread out from her chest. The words of the verse tangled around the images of Shawn: his last breath in the mouth of this creature. She thought of Mack; his life cut short. And of Gracelyn who was shaking beside her now. As the snake opened its maw, teeth glittering in the light, Emily drove the spear into it with all her strength.

He will protect you from the evil one.

The force of the blow shoved her backward. She half spun around, her side hitting the wall behind her. The air whooshed from her lungs but the end of the spear wedged into the earthen floor had been driven deeper into the earth. Emily would have screamed in fright if she could have, as the big snake's mouth yawned open inches from her face. A hot wave of its reeking breath engulfed her.

The moaning hum faded.

The spear was jammed into the roof of the snake's mouth. It poked out of the top of its head. Blood ran in a little river over one of its eyes, but the eye didn't blink. Didn't move.

Emily stared as the snake slid and spiraled downward. Away from Gracelyn and her, onto the floor underneath them. The smaller snakes all lay silently, staring in the direction of the big one with their milky eyes.

The snake's body continued to fall backward. It slid down, down, down, tangled under the stone ledge where they sat. Emily couldn't believe it. She couldn't register what she was seeing. Was it really...?

"Is it...dead?" Gracelyn asked seconds later. Her breath was coming in little pants, her eyes wide.

"I...don't...know," Emily gasped. The air was finally returning to her lungs which burned and ached like she'd swallowed water. She took gasp after gasp of the still-sour air and leaned hesitantly over the edge of the counter.

The big snake lay motionless on the floor. And all the other snakes, with their pale, white eyes, lay facing it, silent and still.

"I think it might be," Emily said. "Oh God," Emily covered her face with shaking, dirty hands. She sobbed but no tears came out. Then, she straightened. "Gracie. Are you okay?"

"What? Yes, I'm fine. I'm fine." Gracelyn's voice, like Emily's, sounded strange and unnatural.

Emily pulled Gracelyn's hand into her own, kissed the back of it and squeezed it hard.

"Mom," Gracelyn said, dazedly. "You...you killed it."

A bubble of laughter—probably hysterical—bubbled out of Emily's throat.

"I think so," she said. "I think I really did. Oh, Gracie," she turned and hugged her daughter. Gracelyn wrapped her arms around her, tentatively at first, then harder until she was really gripping her.

Then the tears came. Emily felt them soaking Gracelyn's shirt. It was over. Thank God, Emily thought, it was really, finally over.

33

EMILY EDWARDS

THE SETTLEMENT

Present Day

I t took hours for Emily to get them out of the basement. It took a long time for the venom to wear off enough for Gracelyn to stand, let alone walk.

"We need to get you to the hospital," Emily said as they rested under a big tree. "They'll need to check you out."

Gracelyn frowned but nodded. "Not yet. Please, just let me rest a little bit longer."

Emily nodded.

"Hey, you saved it?" Gracelyn asked, pointing to Emily's pocket. She glanced down, surprised to see the little brown journal half sticking out of her jacket pocket.

"I'd forgotten all about it," Emily said.

"Let's read it. Maybe it will give us some answers," Gracelyn said. "Help me sit up?"

Emily helped her lean back against the tree trunk, then

opened the cover of the book. It was musty but dry, the
pages yellow and brittle.

"It's old," Emily described it for Gracelyn. "Bits of dried
leather are coming off of the spine." She cleared her throat.
"There's an inscription on the cover page. It says, 'Jerome
Lancaster, and a date, July 12th, 1779.'"

She turned the page and began to read.

*I, Jerome Lancaster, being of sound body and mind do record this
personal missive on the twelfth day of July, 1779. What my pen
records should be taken as fact. I am one of the four founding
fathers of this town. I record this in the hopes that our history and
the choices that led them, will never be repeated.*

*THOUGH WE HAVE KEPT outsiders away, those in the neighboring
town, called "Bondville" have begun to overstep boundaries. We
alone know of the Dark Magic and must keep it from all other
hands. Our ancients have commanded it and it will be hidden
even at the peril of our new homes here. It must be kept sacred. It
must be protected!*

"THE NEXT ENTRY IS DATED," her mother paused. "About five
months later. Same speaker."

*ALAS, what horror have we unleashed? Our founding fathers
have voted and I alone was in distrust of this plan. It is not right.
It is not as the Dark Magic would instruct. But my pleas and
threats have fallen on deaf ears.*

.   .   .

A Gathering has been set. *There is talk among the people of revenge, of justice for those in the town of Bondville for their threats toward us and our way of life. The townspeople threaten us. They do not understand our sacred language. They do not appreciate our power. And they do not know of the serpent god we have created...*

"The ink is smudged here, but," Emily flipped the page. "It continues here."

...will culminate in the destruction of their young. The Gathering ceremony—sacred and holy—yet I fear that it will be the undoing of our little community. The snake god grows larger and more powerful. I fear its power. It breeds on the resentment and fear among our people. 'What will stop it?' I asked the council members. But no one had an answer for me.

My fellow council *members call me a coward, say that I fear our history. But it is not our history that causes me to tremble, but our future. We cannot do this thing and remain as we have been. Our humanity, I fear, will become changed for the worse.*

"The next entry is a week later." A sick feeling rose in her stomach as she skimmed the words before reading them aloud.

It is over. *The children of our enemies are dead. But there is no peace here in our community. Rather, rage and greed and all*

*manner of villainous behaviors have been unleashed. And the
snake god grows larger still...*

"ANOTHER BREAK IN ENTRIES. Now it's two weeks after the last
one," Emily said.

*THERE IS a plague unleashed among us. Not of natural origin. But
a pestilence that will not let us rest. There are now only a handful
of us left. The others...are dead. Not by my hand, though I did sit
watching so in some ways perhaps I am an accomplice? The
snake god is hungry. It devours those who created it. And now it
has broken free of confinement and made a new home for itself up
in the mountain.*

*I BELIEVE the motives of man fuel this serpentine abomination. As
we grow weaker over our desires, it grows stronger and more
powerful. As we kill and seek revenge and hate our brothers, it
feeds and grows fatter still.*

WHAT HAVE WE DONE?

EMILY FLIPPED to the next page but it was blank. She turned
further into the book, looking for more answers, but the rest
of the pages were all empty.

"That's all there is," she said quietly. "Nothing else."

Gracelyn reached out a hand to Emily who took it and
held it weakly in her own.

"Those poor people," Gracelyn said softly. "The people

who lost their kids. Dad's stories...about Bondville. The others who believed. It was real. But how—" Gracelyn began but stopped.

"How what?" Emily

"How did you kill it? If that snake was manifested, created by—" she waved a hand toward the little journal. "In a supernatural way, how could a human kill it?"

Emily cleared her throat. She hadn't told Gracelyn about the Bible she'd been reading or the comfort she'd found in its pages. She knew what her daughter's reaction would be. Emily herself wouldn't believe it if she hadn't experienced it.

"I think it had to do with the Bible verse," Emily said quietly. "It came to me in there. And I repeated it over and over."

"You think a...a Bible verse killed the snake?"

"If it's true that the snake was created in darkness, with evil intents then couldn't it also be possible that it was undone with light? With good intention and love?"

Gracelyn was quiet for a few long seconds.

"I guess," she said finally. "Honestly, none of this makes much sense to me. Not a gigantic snake or a centuries-old curse or Bible verses."

Emily leaned back against the tree closest to her daughter. She looked at Gracelyn. Not Gracie the Spitfire toddler or the sassy kid. Not the rebellious teen who'd stolen her parents' car and crashed it. Instead, Emily saw her daughter —really saw her—maybe for the first time in her life.

"Thank you," Gracelyn said finally, interrupting the quiet. "For saving me. And always loving me, even when I couldn't see it." Her eyes filled up with unshed tears and she blinked hard several times.

Emily smiled and leaned over. She dropped a kiss on her daughter's forehead.

"I do love you, Gracie," she said. "I always have and always will. Now, let's get out of here."

Emily helped her stand and repositioned her daughter's arm, taking on more of her weight.

Emily pointed them in the direction of Bondville.

"Let's go home," she said.

ACKNOWLEDGMENTS

As always, I couldn't have written this book without some serious support. To Pam Irish, Ann Kalinoski, and Angela Lavery: I'm so grateful to have you as my early readers. Your feedback is important and always makes the story stronger. Team Captain, Erin Chagnon, thank you for all the great insights and your ability to make me laugh my way through the list of silly errors and implausible situations you find in the early draft. As always, I appreciate your help and astuteness.

I offer my humble thanks to Helen Baggot, an excellent editor. It's a pleasure to create a book with you. Michele Deppe: what would I do without your help formatting? I appreciate all your patience very much. Thanks also to Bespoke Book Covers for creating another creepy and lovely cover.

To all my friends, family and readers who enjoy these stories and offer your support in so many ways: THANK YOU! Chances are good I would have given up writing a long time ago if not for you. A very special thank you to Ray McClure, a wonderful supporter, and encourager. Your kindness to me and our mutual love of discussing all things art, religion and education are very much appreciated.

And lastly, but certainly not least: my supportive, steadfast and loving husband, Serge. Thanks for keeping me going. You're getting much better at the pep talks! And to my darling boy, Pascal, I'm so proud of you and love seeing how your own creativity and faith continue to flourish.

Most of all, I'm grateful to God for the opportunity to share these stories and use the gifts I've been given.

~Dios Amore~

AUTHOR'S NOTE

The idea of someone who was legally blind climbing a mountain might seem impossible...it's not. This story was inspired in part by the biography, *Blind Courage,* by Bill Irwin and David McCasland. Irwin, legally blind, hiked the entire Appalachian Trail, from Georgia to Maine with his dog, Orient.

I'm always inspired by individuals who do things that to me, feel impossible or at least extremely difficult...like say, hiking the Appalachian Trail while being able to see. More so when the person accomplishing the challenge has to work within the parameters or their disability.

I hope you enjoyed *Under the Mountain,* Book Three of the "Monsters in the Green Mountains," series. Each book in the series can be read as a stand-alone. If you'd like to read the rest of the series or any of my other Vermont-based thrillers, visit www.jpchoquette.me. Plus, you can enjoy a free, creepy short story when you sign up for my newsletter.

Happy reading!